Where Is the Voice Coming From?

Where Is the Voice Coming From?

Rudy Wiebe

McClelland and Stewart Limited

0-7710-8987-2

The Canadian Publishers
McClelland and Stewart Limited
25 Hollinger Road, Toronto

Printed and bound in Canada

Books by Rudy Wiebe

Fiction:

Where is the Voice Coming From? (1974)
The Temptations of Big Bear (1973)
The Blue Mountains of China (1970)
First and Vital Candle (1966)
Peace Shall Destroy Many (1962)

Editor:

Stories from Pacific and Arctic Canada
(1974, with Andreas Schroeder)
Stories from Western Canada (1972)
The Story-Makers (1970)

To L.M.B.C.,
brothers and sisters.

Contents

Scrapbook 13

Tudor King 19

Someday Soon, Before Tomorrow 27

Millstone for the Sun's Day 37

There's a Muddy Road 45

Did Jesus Ever Laugh? 57

All on Their Knees 73

Oolulik 87

Bluecoats on the Sacred Hill of the Wild Peas 103

Along the Red Deer and the South Saskatchewan 113

The Fish Caught in the Battle River 125

Where Is the Voice Coming From? 135

The Naming of Albert Johnson 145

Where Is the Voice Coming From?

Scrapbook

In the darkness under the rafters he awoke to the screaming.

It was like his dream of being crushed by a huge tree and waking up to find his brother's arm lying on him, inert and solid in sleep. But now he had had no dream. Rather, he had felt something a long, long time, as if it stretched back without end into his slumber, even as if he had felt it forever: the leaping rise, the rasping plateau of sound, and then the moaning fall of it down to a whimper, before he awoke and heard it.

All was quiet for a moment after he awoke and these things groped through his thought, when suddenly he knew that David was not in bed beside him. Why wasn't he there? The strangeness of his absence and the sleep-remembered sound – had he heard something after he awoke? – welled fear in him. The straw-tick squeaking, he snuggled over into the big hollow and it was not warm at all. Where was David – *had* he heard – and then he jerked erect, careless of the dark, because the stove-pipe which reached up through the middle of the attic seemed surrounded by light. It was! for a light from below shone up through the opening around the pipe. Then he heard movement there. Were they all up, with the light burning? Perhaps he had heard –

The screaming came again. It occupied his bent body completely, that inhuman scream, as if he and it were alone in a universe; it drowned his brain until he could not hear it for the sound, and then it fell horribly, as if stretched beyond elasticity, down to a burbling moan.

He snatched the quilt up and over, but the half-warm darkness was not enough. He had to find them. His small bare feet were cold on the rough boards as, hunched against the darkness, he felt for the top of the ladder-like stairs near the oblong of grey that showed light below. Then he felt it and slipped down, feet quick on the familiar steps. The moaning had almost died now, and he could hear movement beyond the curtain of the living room. He crept over and pulled it aside.

He did not know what he saw as he stood for a long moment, fear forgotten. It was not that the lamp-light was strong on his sleep-rimmed eyes. Rather he did not know why his big sister Marg, who had lain on the bed in the corner of the living room for months because she had an enlarged heart, his mother said, was now in the middle of the night so stiffly erect in a chair, as if nailed there. And why David and his father should be holding her down. He had never seen her face like that. Like a crumpled paper-doll. Her black hair was stuck in strings over her forehead as his mother wiped her face, and then he saw the clothes-pin gripped in her teeth and the blood oozing from her lips. In the wonder of it he stared, rooted, and suddenly the pain within her tore the shell that held it and he heard the scream again, saw it ripped from her throat and saw the muscles of the men's arms bulge as they tried to hold her in the chair.

The fear numbed him now. He looked here and there as the sound seared him. If it was near David and his father, where – then he felt arms around him. His sister, five years older than himself, sitting crying by the door, clutched him to her.

It was not so long as last time, and he could look up as his father, face beaded with sweat and tears, said desperately, "Mother, we have to do something – we can't stand this," and David, almost maddened, hissing fiercely,

"Do something! *We* can't stand this! Look at her – thinking about yourself!"

And his mother, wiping the tortured face again, saying, "David, don't. That doesn't help. She bites her lips so much when she can't stand it – if we could only stop her burning. Maybe the Samsons – "

"Mrs. Samson would know *something* – get her – or do something. Get Bud to ride and get her."

They noticed him then as he huddled with his sobbing sister, not knowing himself what to do, cry or not. He didn't want to cry in front of David, who said crying was sissy, but Marg seemed to

14

hurt so terribly. And everyone was so different. David said, "Bud, get Prince and ride for the Samsons. Quick!"

His mother bent over him. "I have to go out – I can't stay to see her – Toots, get some colder water and wipe her face. I'll take the lantern, Buddy."

In a rush he was dressed and out in the coolness where the spring frogs croaked hoarsely through the morning dark. He liked to ride, but now – when they were near the barn they heard the scream again but it seemed far away and unattached to him. Like a coyote howl in the night when he lay in bed. He jerked at the door, and the warmth from the horses moved around him. Straining, he reached up and looped the bridle off its peg. The only sound was the horses' breathing in the dark and his mother's half-held sobs as she raised the lantern in the doorway.

"Whoa," he said softly. "Easy, Prince, old boy," as he stroked the black object in the stall. The horse moved over, waking up, and he went into the narrow space murmuring quietly as David had taught him to do at night. The teeth would not open for a bit so he scrambled up on the manger and strained over to lever them apart, slipped the bridle over the flattened ears, snapped the strap, undid the halter shank and, grabbing the long mane, half swung, half jumped to the smooth back.

"Okay Mom."

The light swung away and he backed the sleepy horse out of the stall, wheeled it, and, hanging over the left side, right arm and leg clinging, rode out the low door. He was glad he didn't have to walk out of the black barn.

"What shall I say, Mom? Mom?"

Her voice sounded choked. "Tell them Marg's terribly sick – to come quick and help."

Somehow her expression of those few words made him feel her dread for the first time. Someone, a neutral person, had to share this horrible night with them and he knew then he had to do something so he kicked the reluctant Prince sharply. As the horse moved he could hear her say, "Be careful, my little Buddy," and then her voice fell into prayer. He was so busy getting Prince into a gallop he did not hear the high distant sound reaching after him as he swung through the gate and onto the narrow road.

The clouds raced across the moon and its light flicked over the the landscape as if whipped by a fierce wind. Down among the trees, however, all was still as he heard and felt the rhythmical clop of hooves carry up through him and into the night. With a shudder he knew he didn't like the spruce now. They were too solidly black. And grasping. He kicked Prince hard to get him past the muskeg. Where the moonlight slid out spasmodically, the violet blots of the spruce shadows leaped up and poured around him, and when there was no moon the darkness held all. The last stretch was an opaque tunnel, with the horse's withers rocking up at him, solid and living, in the (he knew abruptly) senseless fear that gripped him; just at the end the scream seemed to stab out of the blackness and he was terrified. But then he twisted the corner out of the forest to where poplars bordered the road on one side and the dull greyness of the Samson field stretched out against the pale, moving sky on the other.

The open was better; his thoughts raced on with the hard-running horse. This was like the dreams of riding through the night for help – all by himself, just as he had read in *Black Beauty*. Not many boys, perhaps not even most men, had ever done this. He'd tell them at school!

There was a clump of trees now, then the wooden bridge over a spring creek that burbled between sloughs filled with croaking frogs. The hoofs clunked hollow twice, and he was over, then in an instant saw the outline of the Samson gate. Prince turned up the lane. The farm-yard lay black and violet under the half-bare moon.

The dogs barked raucously out of their sleep as he slid off. Holding the reins taut, he banged on the door. "Mr. Samson! Mr. Samson!" Except for the dogs, he knew he could not have opened his mouth against the night. He hammered again and again, suddenly desperate for movement from the still house. Then, as he finally stopped for his numb fist and tilted over, panting, suddenly footsteps came. The door creaked.

"Mr. Samson – " he was staring at the long night-dress, "Mrs. – Marg's awful sick. Mom says, come quick, and help. . . . "

"What's wrong?"

"She – she (he did not know what to say) she bites herself and she sits in the chair and David and Dad are holding onto her and – and – "

"Ride home quick, we'll come right away. George – " she was turning to the figure joining her in the lean-to.

He yanked Prince over to the wagon in the yard, scrambled up, jumped to his back and was headed home. He was cold now, and he saw the eastern tree-tops were just tipped, as with gold foil. Prince galloped with a will so he closed his eyes and hung on. The road was endless; the horse seemed to run so hard. He felt shaken apart and once he barely caught himself slipping off in sleep. He did not even see the spruce.

His mother was waiting, alone, in the yard. "She said they're coming, right away," he mumbled. He rode in, unsnapped the bridle, tumbled off, snapped the shank on and, dropping the bridle in the corner, went out. His mother took his arm at the door.

"I went in once, but it's too terrible. Oh my Buddy, she's burning up and I can't do anything. It came just like that – so quickly – and she's burning up!" They were near the wood-pile and she dropped to her knees by the chopping block. He could feel her frantic clasp on his small body as she prayed, the same words over and over.

"Aw, Mom," he said when she choked, crying, "it's – "

He didn't know anything to say. Where was the word to say when his mother was like this. She who could do everything. Then his crying rose and fell with hers at the great unknowing fear, the helplessness he felt through her. The scream in the distance was very weak, and did not come again for a long time.

Suddenly a jingle of harness and, in a moment, the Samsons whirled up. As Mr. Samson tied the horse, Mrs. Samson came to them by the wood-pile and put her arm around his mother. She clutched his hand, sobbing, "She was getting so much better and all of a sudden, in the night – "

"We brought some laudanum – that should help some."

He knew it would be all right. They walked to the house; sleep kept pulling his head over as the house came closer. There was a dark door opening, closing them inside.

In the late morning when he awoke and came downstairs, his mother told him Margaret was dead.

The house did not smell right. Everyone seemed to be struck dumb, and cried unexpectedly. He could not find David anywhere. He did not want to go into the living room; he could not think of anyone as dead.

"Mom," he said, "I want to go to school."

His mother didn't seem to hear him. After she had told him she had turned away and was washing dishes, alone in her grief for the girl she had nursed so long.

He went out, and the early spring sunshine was fresh and good.

No one noticed him as he slipped into the barn, bridled Prince, and rode off.

Yet, somehow, school wasn't right either. When he got there he didn't feel like saying anything about his ride, or even why he arrived during recess. He sat in his small desk in the one-room school and the teacher said, "Grade three, take out your Healthy Foods Scrapbooks." He opened his desk and there, slightly dog-eared and crumpled from much looking, lay the scrapbook. He and Marg had made it for health class. Actually Marg had done all the work; he had just watched. That was why his book had been first in class. On the cover was the bulging red tomato she had cut from the tomato-juice label, and there was the kink she had made when he bumped her because he was leaning so close as she sat propped in bed, cutting it out. He said, almost aloud, "She's dead," and he knew that 'dead' was like the sticks of rabbits he found in his snares.

And suddenly he began to cry. Everyone stared, but he could not stop.

Tudor King

"Will he be all right?" the boy asked again. Against the cold his breathing came in short gasps and his normally round face was pinched together expectantly to the huge parka-ed figure beside him.

"I told you — we'll see when we get there," his brother Frank flipped the reins gently against the flanks of the horses. Encouraged, they butted their way into another drift driven behind the brush skirting the road. "Don't talk. Just stop wriggling, keep the robe up – tight."

Immediately the boy settled back and resolved again not to make another move until they got there. The question, however, ran on through his mind in circular repetition, like Little Black Sambo's tigers around and around the tree. Remembering that naked little fellow, the boy involuntarily hunched lower into the blankets for warmth, eyes squinting at the storm-wasted world. His father had said it had been the worst storm to ever hit the district. For five days the blizzard had whipped the pellet-snow across the land; one evening only the ropes they had strung between house and barn had brought Frank safely in from feeding the stock. But last night when the boy awoke there had been no storm whine. What he heard as he lay, limp from sleep and staring at the red bulge of the heater, was the sad howl of the wolves, hunger-desperate after the storm. He had heard, and felt something finger down his spine even as he curled up more tightly, pulling the wool quilt up and over, and then he had heard his father just beyond the bedroom partition make a sound in his sleep and the long moans had lost their hold and he had lain snug, his eyes wide again to the cheery heater. Abruptly he had remembered the old man, thought of all the after-blizzard nights he must have lain in his sagging cabin, hearing the wolves. With no father to clear his throat in the darkness.

Now, the team plowing steadily ahead, the boy shuddered again. He sensed Frank looking at him and to cover up he rubbed his nose fast with the back of his mitten. Somehow that did not seem enough; he crouched lower in the seat of the cutter and lifted the heavy robe over his head. The musty smell of the cow-hide brought him back to the old man again because that was his cabin smell too. Mixed with some others.

His father had said the old man was already there when they came to their homestead. Probably he had always lived there, bent, scum-grey hair projecting from his face and under his cap, pants held up by twine, stitched together with string, old. On warmer days in spring and summer he shuffled past their farm every week towards the store which was also post office, his hands folded behind his back, a greyish sack held in place by cord over his shoulder. And at his heels followed the dog, small, brownish, and always bald at varying spots from his truceless battle with fleas. Like the other children of the settlement, the boy stared at the stooped figure almost apprehensively from behind a tree or barn-corner. The name, hissed at bedtime, was enough to quiet any restless youngster.

But once, last summer, the boy had faced him. On a long Sunday afternoon the boy and two friends, daring each other into a corner beyond their courage, had inched up to the cabin where the old man lived. Someone, with gritted teeth, knocked. And then the door squeaked open and they were inside where the litter, gathered home over years in the greyish sack, left them barely room to shuffle their feet. The dog, squatting on the sack-heaped bedstead too, looked more miserable than ever, but something had happened to the old man. In the darkness under the robe the boy, now as then, saw him in awe. And heard his voice.

"Think I'm in bad shape, huh? You," jabbing a finger at the tallest of the three, "you taken history?" He said it as if there were only one bit of history to be known and it could be taken like a pill.

Henry nodded hastily.

"It says the Tudors was once kings of England. Eh!" The last was not a question; his whole body jerked as he shot it out.

20

Henry, whose head was still bobbing slightly from the previous question, said quickly, "Uh-huh!" because that was one bit he did seem to know.

"Well, what's my name?" The boys could say nothing, quite floundered that the old man should ask such a thing. Even the dog had stopped scratching. "Eh!"

Henry ventured, very gently, "Mr – Tudor."

"Eh!" The ejaculation snapped at them like a whip; in the gathering wonder of that moment the three suddenly comprehended. Under the robe, the boy could again see the flash of the grey eyes and again he was mesmerized. "That means I come from them same Tudors that was kings of England. You know what that means?" The voice, not creaking now but great, "I'm a Tudor. I should be king of England."

As if suddenly aware of their numb comprehension, the old man relented a little, but the flame in his eye did not die. "Now I ain't saying I'm against the King. I ain't really, no, only I don't think he's running the war right. Look at what that Hitler's doing to the people. Even bombing them! I ain't against him, but if George was to come out from England and say, 'Tudor, will you take over?' why, I wouldn't refuse him. Eh!"

As on that summer day, the boy heard no more of the voice but in the musty, seeping coldness under the robe he again saw the old man before him. And the dingy flesh obvious through the rags, the bedraggled whiskers, the rotting shoes, even the dog with his ceaseless scratch, were transformed. If before him was the nadir of humanity, the flashing eyes and the compulsive spirit moving there revealed the stuff of majesty. The lined face was no longer directed toward the palpable ambitions of youth; no longer toward an actuality or even a probability. Whatever had crushed any fulfillable ambition had not been able to erase a fragment of history, or prevent it from blossoming in the failing mind of the old man.

The boy had not actually known this on the last summer afternoon as he and his friends stood dumb in the cabin. He did not even know it now under the robe on his way to see how the old man had weathered the storm; if asked directly, he could have shaped no words to explain himself. He simply knew what he had seen in the wreck before him, and the two miles home had vanished under his feet as he sped to tell all he could put in words: I saw a king! And the disappointment struck him again as he remembered how Frank had laughed.

"Ah Andy. That's his dream. Told me years ago. Dream – what else can he do, now?"

He stood sullen in the warm dust of the barnyard. The Tudors *had* been kings of England; it was in a book at school. And the old man's name *was* Tudor. So he must be from the same family, and so the throne belonged as much to him as King George VI. And the way he had looked and the way he had spoken –

Frank put down the book he was reading and leaned back against the haystack. "Sorry Andy, I didn't think you really believed him." He looked over the trees into the sky and added slowly, "But you're almost ten. You've got to learn sometime that you can't believe everything. It's okay to dream about chasing wolves and flying planes – every boy does – but you can't go around believing every old tramp that says he's a king. Even if his name happens to fit something, four hundred years ago."

Seeing the boy stare wordlessly at the ground, he insisted, "kid, you can tell. He's not really right anymore, up here. He's lived alone and with that dog too long. A man can become low and cheap if he just lives with himself too long. He can become no man at all. How can a man live as he does – in a shack full of junk and that filthy runt. That's what you saw. Listen. Just last week Ted Martin was missing some eggs again. He had a good idea where they were going, so when he met old Tudor on the road he said, 'You know, I've been losing eggs out of my barn again.'

"'Oh,' says old Tudor, 'Say, there must be a snitcher around. Just yesterday I was missing some – '

"'Yah,' Ted interrupted, 'but I'm fixing him. I'll plant some poisoned eggs in that barn and we'll see what's what.'

"Ted said Tudor's eyes got all big and scared, 'Hev Ted, you wouldn't do a thing like that to an old friend, would you?'"

After a moment Frank said heavily, "All these years he's lived alone, in dirt. Too long. All the truth and pride in him – everything's rotten away. What can you believe him?"

But no logic or facts could budge the idea caught in the gleam of the old man's eye as he sat enthroned among the sacks of his bed. The boy could no more deny it than he could understand it. But it was there.

He heard Frank shout "Haw!" and he felt the cutter lurch to the left. He thrust his head above the robe; they were turning off the main road up the drifted track to the cabin now, the greys steaming, heaving themselves forward together. The jack-pine and scrawny outline poplars crowded closer here. It was too cold for wind or even clouds; there was just one massive inhuman concentration on cold. The sunlight blazing on the drift-driven snow only added ironical emphasis.

But the cold, sting as it might, could not hold his thoughts. *Around the copse and then we'll see,* he thought, keeping even the cold at arm's length. *Just around the corner. A few more steps – that one more big drift, and there it will be –*

Only it was not. When they rounded the last pine they saw no cabin in the clearing. The boy jerked to his feet. Where the cabin should have been hunched in the lee of a small hill there was only the straight waste of a giant drift that had levelled the clearing to lose itself at the edge of the spruce. Then, his eyes skipping back over the drift, he saw the bit of stove-pipe sticking up and he knew that the wind had only buried the shack and that beneath the hard surface it was snug and – then he looked at the stove-pipe again.

"Frank," he said.

His brother was standing too, huge, his weathered face rimmed by the frost on his parka. "Yah," he said.

The horses fought their way a bit closer, then halted at a word. Frank muttered, "Hang on here," giving the boy the reins, and stepped out to pull the blankets over the hot horses. "I agreed to watch him, but the Mounties can't blame me. Not for a five day blizzard."

"Frank – "

"Stay in the cutter! Get under there and stay warm. Y'hear!" The boy, knowing his brother was rough because he had just said what he need not have said, and yet having been compelled to say it though useless, sat down slowly and watched him bull himself into the deepening snow. From this angle the boy could see that the wind had eddied the snow clear within a few feet of one side of the cabin, leaving a curving rift in the drift. He saw the iceless glass of one small window; he looked at the stove-pipe. No smoke. He remembered the look of the old man. He dropped the reins and was out, his legs churning along the straggled trail. Frank wheeled at him, mouth open to thunder, then after an instant stooped without a word to continue clearing the door.

The inner door ground a cracking protest on its leather hinges. Beyond the flash of snow the interior was black as Frank pushed back his hood and stepped in. He completely blocked the opening, but the boy, hunching over, slipped past his legs. As he stood there facing the gloom he could feel the old trunk against his leg and he knew from the shadows that the clutter of pottery and worn-out harness of the summer before was still upon it. Through a corner of the east window the sunlight now managed a faint reflection, outlining in ragged silhouette the heaps of things crowding the room. The stove-pipe stood above the hump of the heater against the middle of the low ceiling. The boy's mittened hand reached up to the edge of Frank's parka in the silence of their breathing.

"Uh – Tudor," Frank cleared his throat gruffly. Then more loudly, "Tudor, you here?" His voice bounced about.

After a moment Frank started into the room. "He saw a hundred storms – had enough wood for four days if he skimped." He leaned forward in the gloom about the heater. "Maybe he tried to go out for more – there's none h – Oh."

He straightened instantly, brushing away the boy's hand. "Andy, you better get back to the cutter, and . . . " but there was no need to finish. More accustomed to the half-light, the boy had already seen the figure curled tight against the heater, the back cramped against it as though to plead some touch of warmth from its rigid flank. They both leaned closer as sunlight from the door fell on the granite face. An icicle of saliva had frozen the mouth and beard to the floor.

Frank said, "Wonder, where's the dog."

The boy, still gripping the parka, pointed.

"Huh?" Frank's glance moved slowly around the room, ending on the bed bare to its rope springs. His hands fumbled slightly as he thrust his mitts more firmly onto them, then, with an abrupt movement he bent down. Rigidly, as a welded iron framework, the whole shape moved. He half-straightened and said strangely. "No weight to it." Then quickly he reached in and pulled the dog from where it had been cradled, hugged, in the nest of rags. It seemed at that moment to be turning stiff. Even as Frank pushed something aside and eased it to the floor, the hairless limbs stretched rigid also.

Frank said slowly, "He tried his best for the dog. Knowing we'd come when the storm dropped, Old Man Tudor."

Then he suddenly turned. The boy felt himself lifted up in his brother's strong arms, held close as he had not been since he was a

24

small child. But he did not find that strange. Something was breaking through his numbness, painful and wet, and he pushed his face against his brother's hard, cold shoulder; as if he were already remembering his own fierce happiness at once having recognized the fleeting stuff of human majesty.

Someday Soon,
Before Tomorrow

It was the first day of May. The spring sunlight lit the patchwork flatness of Manitoba countryside, the straight roads and the twisting rivers, the pinpoint farmyards and the clustered towns, the bare lines of the shelterbelts and the sprouting whiteness of willows along the creek-beds. It spread like a beneficence over the winter-wan land, but it also revealed four men grouped on a municipal road who were talking almost fiercely, their arms swinging out at a wide expanse about them that should have lain black and heavy with expectation. But there was only the level gleam of water.

A small truck halted behind the column of vehicles strung on the road's shoulder and a heavy-set man stepped down. The other men silenced and, one by one, turned toward him. A tall lean man said, "Morning, I G."

"Morning Walter, morning men," the newcomer's glance slid over the weather-hardened faces nodding in greeting. "I couldn't just drive past friends. You're gathering early."

A man in bibbed overalls snapped, "You've as little to joke about now as most of us will in a couple hours. You expect the water to rise this fast?"

I G drawled, "Can't say I'd have done much if I had, Harry."

Walter Kostiuk turned impatiently. "We're not laughing, I G. See that?" His bony finger jabbed at the two eddies in the water below them in the ditch. "Them two two-foot culverts have been over their tops since last night. It'll keep on backing up on your and my land now, and the same thing's already started on Harry's on the next road. And it'll keep on like that for another mile

27

before it gets to the Granmere ditch. Everyone of them damn culverts is too small. Before the marsh is drained we'll all of us be three-quarters under water!"

Eyes intent on his own fencepost that poked a foot of its length and one of its three wires above the water, I G said, "I didn't vote for Royer. And I didn't get on the list for haying rights on the marsh."

An uncomfortable shuffle stirred the farmers. It was true enough they had eagerly followed Jake Royer when he ran for reeve on an 'Improve our Municipality' platform.

"Huh! Royer!" snorted another, and spat. "He's watched too much TV. Even with lotsa spring water we used to have only little puddles along the creek and the marsh could just stay where it was –"

"Ah shut up, Jim," growled someone.

"Yah," Walter said. "We know now, all of us. What are we gonna *do* now?"

They stood, hard bodies bent, eyes brooding on the silt-scummed water that chuckled as it whirled into the narrow crib of the culverts and sprang away at its release, easing down the imperceptible fall of the land until a mile further south another pair of culverts too tight for its girth would spread it relentlessly over the crumbly soil, building up pressure to squeeze it faster and faster through the steel strictures until they too were buried and the water would gurgle into another eddy and ram its way through to glide sedately on. And after another such delay of some hours or days or perhaps weeks it would ease itself into the huge Granmere Drain to be led, without discomfort, to where the Red River squirmed across the plain and through the city and around oak and poplar bends to the immensity of Lake Winnipeg. Eventually some stray stubble now rimming the curve of the eddies before them would reach the lake, but the men had no thought for that. What they needed to know was, hedged by the physical circumstances before them and the legal ones all realized were there but which few of them could have pinpointed, leave alone countered, how they could drain and dry their land fast enough so they could do what farmers are meant to do: seed a crop. And they looked not to Walter Kostiuk, who could and would speak for them when the time came, but to I G Loring, under whose careless surface, somewhere, lay the agility of thought and comprehension which, could they but prod it, might puncture the dam of their dilemma. And, oddly enough, they all knew that his being in that dilemma deeper than any of them at the moment was not the factor which would stir him.

I G said, "Did you call Royer?"

"Yah," Walter replied. "The council's meeting this afternoon, but he doesn't think they can do much. They've no money – the big road contract was signed last week."

"Sure," I G laughed and his voice rose to mimic level. " 'I tell you, farmers of La Crosse, our municipality could and *will* be the finest and most progressive municipality in Manitoba. We'll make people sit up and take notice. We have the farmers; we have the land and', " he made a grand gesture, '—now we have the water!' "

No one guffawed. Jim said harshly, "Damn it, I G, will you quit horsin – " he stopped for a black car with a white door had sighed to a halt beside them. The officer in it looked up at them but did not get out.

"Good day, men." All nodded in greeting. "Anything wrong?" They did not move; no one said anything. The policeman looked right and studied the water pouring from the culvert into the watercourse that led south across the land, the creek marked here and there by half-submerged willows. He turned to the farmers, but they had not moved so he backed his car slightly to see the water sprawling over the fields to the north. With a jerk he pulled even with the glowering men. "Culverts can't take it eh? Does this happen every year?"

Walter said, gesturing, "No. Just since that so-called drain was dug last summer."

"I see." The policeman was obviously trying to be understanding but the belted elegance of his voice did not help him. "Why didn't they put in bigger pipes?"

Walter flicked his cigarette over the car-hood into the ditch as I G drawled, "Farmers hardly tell engineers from Winnipeg what to do."

The policeman looked up sharply at I G's bland, direct glance, then at the others who stood, sullen, eyes on their boots or far over the fields. "You're being put in a bad way, all right," he said; his radio sputtered and he listened for a moment, then flicked it off, "but I wouldn't get any quick notions about pulling up a few culverts to stop the back-up. Destroying municipal property is a

29

criminal offence." His glance locked with I G's, who smiled abruptly.

"Wel-l-l now. When you drove up, sir, we were in a slight quandry as to what could be done. But if, without even leaving your car, you could help us solve our problems – "

Flicked to the raw, the officer interrupted, "What's your name?"

"I G Loring."

"Where do you live?"

"Sure – " after a slight pause, "right over there, beyond the big puddle in the house among the trees."

"It was to you I was talking then. Don't get any foolish ideas on how to – "

"Hold on one damn minute," Walter Kostiuk was beside the car in two strides. "You're new here, but just what kind of a stupid accusation is – "

I G's big hand was on his shoulder, "Walter, don't be rough on our friend. He is doing his duty. I'd be kinda peeved too if every workin' day of my life I hadta say things to people they didn't like, all the time wearin' puckered britches with a yellow stripe down my leg."

The tension split with a roar from four muscular throats. The officer, his face black with anger, said rigidly, "The Mounted Police brought law to the West in 1874 and – "

"Sure," I G said, "and my grandfather broke this half section with a walking plow in 1888. History doesn't need a uniform." The big farmer smiled again, and now his smile was broad, warm. "I'm sorry if I had to bother you – ah – Constable Ribbing, isn't it? We're under a bit of pressure right now."

"All right," Ribbing ducked his head a moment, then put the car in gear. "I can see it's rough. Just remember what I said."

When the black car had vanished in the dust of the road the farmers crowded around I G, voices urgent. "Listen," I G battered them down, "it won't work. People'd come driving along and get wrecked – hurt – "

"We could put up road blocks at the sections," Jim interrupted.

"Coupla days open running and the whole mess woulda moved into Granmere," rumbled another.

"You heard him – it's illegal! Wait till the council meeting this afternoon."

Walter spoke at last, bitterly, "They won't do nothing. We know you don't care much for farming – probably laugh if you couldn't get on the land for a year – but we've got to work together; every hour a few more acres of my land is under, and Harry's is starting, and soon – "

"You want to try pull this thing up with your bare hands?" I G turned away. "At least give Royer a chance. One day won't make that much difference." He walked back to his truck, but the others only stared after him. As he idled by them I G leaned from the cab and said softly, "You want some inside dope? With that new road cut-off, its only forty miles to Winnipeg. We could open a resort. Complete with mucky-loam beaches!"

But there was no grudging smile even on I G's face late that afternoon when he hung up the phone and went out again. The municipal council was over its head in commitments; it could only try for a court action against the engineers which, Walter had assured him grimly, Rick Wenman the lawyer had said could take months, perhaps years, to prove because the drain followed a natural watercourse. I G studied the dike he had spent the afternoon building about the barn, then looked at the water creeping but inevitably advancing up the pasture. He had not thought it could come so high. The cows were huddled in one trampled corner.

He had driven them into the higher loafing yard and was closing the gate when Georgie came running up the lane from the road.

"Hi!" I G shouted.

The boy dropped his lunch-kit on the house-path and ran up to the barn. "Daddy, will we get flooded?"

I G smiled down into his anxious face. "It's started, but it won't rise much higher. It'd run over the south road first."

"But what about the land?"

"It won't reach the house, and the barn's okay with that dike, see. The water won't get at us."

"But the land," Georgie insisted, "it's almost all under water. All the kids in the bus yelled when they saw it. Ours and Mr. Kostiuk's land – "

I G said quietly, "Maybe we won't have any crop this year. You better feed your rabbits; I put them up in the loft, out of the way."

Georgie was studying him, small face pinched in concentration. "Aren't you going to do *something*?" he asked.

"There's too much water for the culverts, that's all." I G gestured. They were in the barn now, and abruptly the boy turned and began climbing up the ladder to the loft. But his look seemed to hang there in the familiar gloom of the barn and I G sensed himself forced back, with a sudden clarity, upon himself. There had been a time when he really wanted to do something. He had a vision for a great new breed of wheat and it had been barely begun when, within days of each other, the news came of his brother's fall at Dieppe and his father's death, and grandfather Loring had come to the university, sharp eyes glittering under his bristle of white hair, "Isaac, you have to take over the farm." So he had come back to the farm, to the land his grandfather had won from wilderness, to the huge stone house his grandfather had built and at which he was now staring through the barn door. He had done all the many things that had to be done, year after year, and in the busy, easy circle of the years he kept on; he did not particularly like farming, but neither did he particularly dislike it either. If the crop was poor one year, it would probably be better the next; the work was easy; one could avoid strain. And now, in the eyes of his son he had begun to comprehend that year by year the belief which every human must embody if he is to see himself as more than a trace of ink on income-tax records had shrunk in him until, even now when he was finally, abruptly, forced to face the thought head-on, momentarily it seemed less than an inanity; a spasm of electrons flitting amok over his neural connections.

As in a trance he walked out and stared past the corner of the house, across the water that lay master over the land. An unwonted, gut-clutching oath welled as if it would burst in him. God knew he had never wanted the farm! George was to have it! He could now easily rationalize why he had come when he did not want to, under the numbness of the deaths, under the will of his grandfather, and why through the years it became inevitable to simply stay, to work hard physically, and flap a few more self-concocted jokes. And now the water had cornered him.

A hand touched him, and he looked down, at his son smiling

wanly. In the very line of the jaw he could see his grandfather. As they stood, motionless a moment, I G could hear as if it were a physical voice: "That forty down by the creek's good land. A bit low, but full of silt. I saw that soon as I got here in '88. First year – first breakin'. I walked that plow through the buffalo chips and your grandma drove the oxen. Land never touched by iron since God made her. She was a good woman. . . . " The story's warm cadences spoke themselves in his mind, complete to the strange land-woman intertwine the old man always wandered into, the patriarch who he knew bestrode his life like a colossus to nail him to this particular bit of earth, now inundated, helpless.

His son's face had disintegrated in his comprehension, but he could feel the boy's shoulder under his hand. I G shook his head, several times. "Com'mon," he said, and they went together into the massive house. Elaine, his wife, looked up from the kitchen stove as she heard him speak quietly into the telephone: "Walter? Yeah. Yeah. I'll be over in fifteen minutes."

It was almost midnight before they were ready to try. An overcast hid the night sky and the water lapped high on the road shoulder, unheard now over the idling tractors. The road surface was broken wide along the line of the two culverts and I G, dressed again, his head wrapped in a heavy towel, waggled his torch at Walter, then aimed it down at the exit ends. One tractor revved, the cables tightened with groaning hoist. I G tensed forward, but nothing moved. He signalled faster; the tractor's roar deepened; he dropped his light, seized a pick and sprang into the rip above the near culvert. In a frenzy he struck again and again along the ribbed curve of the steel, trying to jar it loose, his huge arms driving the pick down unerringly in the murky light. The towel-end slid over his face and he knocked it from his head. The tractor was grinding down, stalling nearly, when the thing stirred under his feet. He backed a step and struck again with all his strength. A suck smacked on the night; I G staggered, then leaped aside as one and the other culvert scraped and heaved up like gigantic mucky worms spouting into the darkness.

"Georgie!" I G bellowed above the noise, grabbing his light and waving. The other tractor laboured, but the road's hold was broken and with a whooosh! the still submerged in-takes of the culverts broke its surface. The tractors backed slowly, and the two thirty-foot pipes lay on the road, bridging the gaps. For a moment the wall of earth between their former beds held against the flood, then piece by piece it collapsed, vanished, and a ten-foot crest of unleashed water charged through.

The tractors ceased and the scrape of cables being unslung could be heard in the calm above the singing water. Walter Kostiuk emerged on the far side. "Your idea worked good! First heave."

"It was close for a bit," I G's hand fell to his son's shoulder. "Nice work."

Walter said into the quietness, "Handled that tractor like a veteran. Make a good farmer some day."

"He is one already," I G returned, even as they heard the putter of a motorcycle behind them. In a moment, Jim Magyar drew up.

"Hey, you got her up okay, eh?"

"Sure. How about you?"

"Slick as a whistle! She's open straight to Granmere. And every crossin's blocked."

"Good," I G said. "Then we'll just sit here and let it run." At his feet the gap was almost brimming with black, slightly undulating water. "Get that other towel from the cab, Georgie. The one I had is heading for the lake."

The sun was well up when they heard the first car approach. I G roused in the back of his pick-up, got out, and joined Walter leaning against its fender. The second fence wire was visible now, draped with soggy stubble gleaming in the level sunlight. Walter slowly rolled a cigarette.

Ribbing was out of his car and around the tractor before the dust settled. Tall in shiny knee-boots, he studied them across the running water. "So you wouldn't listen. Was that your one-way I had to scrape around at the intersection, Kostiuk?"

The big rumpled farmers returned his look without expression. Walter finally said, "We've got nothing to say to you."

Ribbing's face stiffened. "All right. That's the way it will be." He pulled out a notebook and went around the tractor, striding off distances, sketching, making notes. He crossed on the culverts; his tone as he worked was almost conversational. "I've been on the radio to headquarters. The attorney general will lay what charges he sees fit against you and your friends south of here. I'm impounding every vehicle obstructing public roads, and Reeve

34

Royer is already getting a crew to make these roads passable again. You want to say anything, now?"

Suddenly, into their silence, Georgie's head appeared at the truck window. His eyes drooped, sleep-heavy. "Hello!" Ribbing said, astonished. "What's your name!?"

The boy looked quickly at I G, then away across the water.

The officer's voice was tight. "All right," he said. He clambered back to his car and began speaking rapidly into the radio.

Reeve Royer arrived some time after a crew of men with trucks and a caterpillar tractor had pulled up. The foreman did not look at the two farmers across the gap leaning against the pick-up, but set his men to work pulling Walter's tractor down the road. The reeve, however, balanced his precarious way over the culverts, his face suffused.

"Boys, boys, what have you done! Roads torn up for three miles! All this expense! The west farmers have to haul their eggs and milk to town. How – "

Walter spat. "Stow it, Jake."

"But boys, you can't rip – "

"We just did."

As Royer stood, gesturing wordlessly, the roar of the caterpillar burbled down. Someone yelled,

"Hey! Get that kid off there!"

All turned, and stared. The crew had hitched to the culverts to lift them from their straddle and down into the road again. Only as they stepped back and the cat was about to hoist did they see Georgie. He sat astride one culvert. If it moved, he would slip into the racing water.

Ribbing pushed between the workman. "All right, all right. Get him off there!"

I G peered at his small son, bent and clutching. He said nothing.

The policeman strode to the edge of the rip. "Loring! What's the matter with you! Get him off!"

Even Walter looked at I G then, puzzled. I G had come forward a little, but an odd smile shaped his lips as he looked over his son at the officer. The water ran, silent, impenetrable, under the boy's feet.

"I G," Royer squeaked.

"What the goddamn hell!" Ribbing's control broke and he stepped onto the culvert. But before he could advance more than one unsteady step I G was on the other end and in the instant they confronted each other, teetering, balancing on the mucky roundness, glaring. The cat, its cable taut, chortled almost humanly. Then I G touched the boy's shoulder.

"Com'mon son," he said.

Someone charged through the workmen, gasping, waving a press camera. "Officer! officer! just a sec – would you – "

Ribbing was off the culvert on the instant. "No! Get the hell outa here, you!"

Across the tear I G and Walter looked at each other, then at the cursing reporter. "The man wants a story," I G gestured. "We'll see you, Walter. We're going home."

He and Georgie walked up the road together, past the truck and tractor which, though already impounded, could not actually be possessed until the road was closed, and when they turned from the road and started across the field for the house among the trees they heard the culverts splash behind them. They trudged over the plowed land, their feet sinking in its soft, warm blackness. Their eyes found the wide line of the water's retreat and the land, opening itself completely to the sun. And they were laughing, together.

Millstone for
the Sun's Day

Most of the people seemed to be already on the docks when the boy and his parents arrived, but the press parted swiftly for them. Without hesitation the boy passed down the long dock, the ladies smiling and the men reaching to pat his head, to where the boats lifted easily in the quick morning sunlight. Turning on the last quay, he saw the Yacht. Its white with imperial black piping burned under the solstice sun and, not quite able to believe it, he turned with a laugh to his mother just behind him.

"Mom, can I really ride on it?"

And his father's hand came down on his shoulder with his deep voice, the people all about them quiet and looking, "Joey, just go ahead – over there. We can't be late."

But the boy was looking at his mother still. Usually when he asked her a question his father did not answer. When the boy had come into the kitchen that morning to find the porridge steaming in his bowl but with the unexpected delight of brown sugar beside it, his father had been saying,

"Mary, it's better now than maybe later. You've never said anything against it until – "

But his mother, usually so gentle and quiet, her back stiffly turned and her hands slicing bananas – brown sugar and bananas both on porridge in one day, hey, this was really a holiday – interrupting fiercely, "We don't *have* to let them!"

His father stood rigid as at a blasphemy. "What – Mary – what in all the almighty world – not *have* to?" his voice hanging on incredible pitch, the sunlight in the big-windowed kitchen gleam-

37

ing on the hair of his half-lifted, abruptly paralysed arm. Then he saw the boy in the doorway. "Joey! We didn't even hear you. And dressed already! Ready to go."

"Uh-huh – we better hurry, huh, for the ride?"

His father was smiling, bending to him, swinging him aloft so his head almost touched the ceiling, his father was so tall. The boy cried with delight as he swung up and over, and then he was plopped down facing the steaming porridge. He turned to his mother, laughing. "Mom, we can all ride the Yacht 'cause it was me drew the Lottery. At the meeting-house, eh Mom?"

But his mother did not turn or speak. When she moved at last, placing the tiny bowl of sliced bananas beside his porridge, she sat down beside him, her features tight and stiff, as now on the dock, but her eyes, now bunched against the direct sun, distorting even more her lovely face. The boy did not like her frown. She was always too happy for frowning; rather, singing in the kitchen, shaping towers and boats with his building blocks, walking in the Windy Woods and naming the birds flicking high on the tips of the ferns. Now, suddenly, the boy twisted from under his father's hand and tugged at her dress. "Mom, don't you *want* to ride in the Capitular's Yacht?"

She bent swiftly, her summer skirt flaring out like a dark blot and she was hugging him tight against her breast, silently. Over her shoulder he saw the dark lanes of the people up the lift of the dock, their pale faces turned stiff in their smiles against the dead-blue sky. His mother shivered, and he pushed back.

"Mom, shouldn't I of pulled the Lottery yesterday?" It was incomprehensible. He could remember the disappointment of his friend, Eric, behind him in the line and all the people in the meeting-house waving and clapping for him, the Capitular's hand holding his high to show the mark, the clapping hands flickering everywhere so that he could not see his parents though he knew exactly where they were from watching them as he inched forward in the long line. For an instant only he saw his father's black onyx ring flash in the sunlight from the great arched window in the rhythmic clapping at his winning draw. He was looking at his mother's face now, but her eyes avoided him. And then between the people beyond the sheen of her hair he caught a flash of white and he looked up. A slim white figure came down the dock, floating without sound or seeming motion, the gold-and-crimson ribbon across its breast merging with the crimson of the cantors he knew following.

"Mom!" the boy jogged her shoulder, "Look – look! It looks – just about, all dressed up, like – " he stopped, his recognition shimmering away, then, "isn't it – like Miss Grierson? Look!"

His father's hand fell on his shoulder. "Joey, stand over here, where we belong," and he was hustled to the very edge of the quay where the Yacht waited, motionless as a castle in the water. Past his father's black trouser-leg the boy saw the long bent line of red figures and hats ebbing down between the people and heard the gentle sound that wavered, rising and falling, in the still air, a sound as he had never heard from them before though he had gone since before he could remember, as everyone once a week, and heard them chant in the rood-loft.

"Dad," the boy tugged at the trouser. "What're they singing?"

His father's hand slid over his mouth, the wide ring clicking against his teeth, and he could only look as the flaring baldachin of the Capitular emerged at the head of the dock, flashing red-gold, and the procession stopped and parted, and at long last, in the rising sound, the Capitular at the head of the Lesser Capitulars moved down through the dividing ranks of the cantors to stand beside Miss Grierson in the middle of the dock before the boy and his parents.

The Capitular's benign smile broadened. "Joey." His voice was so deep in the motionless air. "Come forward please." The boy had no time to look to his mother. His father's hand was at his back and he was under the Capitular's raised palm. "Joey. You won the Lottery last evening. Therefore you are our special guest today. We will ride in the Yacht together to Sun Rock, and then perhaps around the island. Will you like that?"

Directly facing the Capitular, the question of what every child on the island dreamed of doing stirred a vague apprehension in the boy, for there was something – and then he forgot not only the correct words but also the bow for suddenly he knew and he spoke without thinking,

"Sir, your Highest – but – but there aren't my friends here."

From the low gasp of the people he knew his breach of whatever was correct and shrank back even as the laugh rumbled above him.

"Of course. But all your little friends *know* you are going with us. On the Yacht. They have all gone to the picnic at the Garden in the Valley, like you did on this day last year. But you are the special one, the only child," the hand was on his head now, the great form bending over him, "that can come on the Yacht. Because you drew the Lottery. Now, don't you like that?"

This time he remembered, and bowed. "Yes. Your Highest."

The hand lifted from his head and the sound of the cantors belled. The boy stood motionless, as they all, eyes on the gold slashing of the Capitular's robe, hearing,

> *The shepherd heard the sheep alway*
>   *High hummocked humitry*
> *The day of wrath to scath shall pass*
>   *High seared in scarify*

The diagonal gold and crimson on white of the other figure before him drew the boy's eye. So very close now, he could recognize Miss Grierson even less than from far away. Her face was immobile, as if caked in something not her own skin, and her eyes, which had laughed only days before with him and Eric building sandcastles in the schoolyard now stared away as through all the people and over the water and through the very sun itself. He stared at her in turn, the Capitular's long intoning above his head not moving him from his amazement. Then abruptly he was wheeled about and, as he twisted for one more look, his father's voice said, "Joey," and he had to turn.

Wonder of wonders to the boy, he walked up the short gangplank first, followed by his parents. And at the head of the gangplank, beard almost brushed into order, stood the old man who sunned himself day after day in the park across the street from the school. No child knew his name, or ever talked about him; no child had ever seen him do anything, but his standing there at rigid attention was merely a minor amazement as the boy and his parents, followed by the Capitular under his baldachin, stepped aboard. In a moment the deck was filled, the motors vibrated, and they were out on the water, smoothly, as if unmoving in their dignity.

No one said a word; motionless their faces sat upon their bodies like blocks. The boy squirmed, trying to look between, around them –

"Joey." The Capitular's voice stung him to stiffness. "You wish to explore the Yacht?" He had not and could not say it but the Capitular, seated in the circle of the Lesser Capitulars and the cantors, seemed to pluck out his thought. The gentle voice continued, "Yes. They always do. You are our guest – go."

The boy's mother, the only other person seated, was holding the boy's hand tightly. But when he looked at her, she nodded hastily. "Yes. I – I'll stay here – now." For an instant he was disappointed. But how often had he dreamed of exploring the largest, the most beautiful vessel on the island! He was gone, slipping between the people. The tall masts where the flags curled and stiffened in the breeze of their motion; the black-bronze railing; the polished wall of the wheelhouse where high above through the window glinted the skipper's glasses; the coiled ropes like barrels; the boy saw it all, and all was wonder. Finally he shouldered back, through the cluster of cantors and for a moment a press of skirts stopped him. And voices.

" – but I'm askin' yuh, why her? You'd think, of all the – " said a young feminine voice, but another interrupted,

"Look kiddo, don't bother. It never makes no difference. None. Just do what you're told."

"Well, it's a shame. And don't it make yuh think, huh?" the other insisted.

"I don't think. It never – " but the boy was pushing between them and the voice shifted, "Oh – it's Joey."

As the boy moved to avoid them the first girl stepped suddenly into his path. "Say, you're seeing the big Yacht. That's nice. Look at the view, over here," and her long bare arm was pulling him and he reluctantly ducked his head below the railing to look as she bent to him. "See the town. Looks nice, don't it, with all the nice tall buildings. And look, over there there's the boat factory." She was pointing in what he vaguely sensed was a kind of flurry, keeping his eyes away from the Yacht. "And doesn't your father work – ain't he a director at the factory – see, over there – "

He had not followed her finger for the flotilla of small boats following had held him. All the boats of the island seemed spread behind the Yacht, bumped full of tiny people, cutting through the water in their wake, but he looked them at the tall chimneys of the factory. "Uh-huh," he said. "Sometimes he takes me along to his office or we look at the motors – " his voice trailed away. "Where's the smoke?"

"There's never no smoke today. See, everybody's here, coming with us." She was erect, gesturing vaguely, pushing him ahead between several girls, and then he was behind an air-funnel, momentarily alone. From deep within the ship rose a muffled throb and he could imagine the great motors running easily, motionless as rocks in their unseeable spinning. With a twist he pried himself between the people again.

And then he saw Miss Grierson. She was sitting, clustered about by girls all dressed, as he suddenly understood the girl talking to him had been, in white but without the band of gold and crimson over their breasts. He wanted to step forward, to tell her – but he saw that she looked even more strange and rigid, sitting so motionless. His mother, now Miss Grierson. A pennant snapped high on the mast above him; he wished suddenly, overwhelmingly, that Eric was there.

He did not want to explore any more. But pushing to find his way back he came upon the old bearded man in a little gap away from everyone leaning over a great block of iron by the railing. The boy looked at it, for it seemed very familiar, but he could not quite decide what it was while the old man muttered to one of the Lesser Capitulars who was hunched down trying to work a rope through one of the innumerable holes in the iron.

" – aint't nothin' what it usta be. Naw sur. In the old days. Usta climb up there, before the sun come up, spend all night climbing, up the trail, through the dark with damn few torches. Just climb. And gettin' them up there was a job. Ha! But everything's gone soft, new stuff, and floating along in boats! Not like we usta climb, *before* sunrise."

The younger man looked up, face flushed. "Is that well tied, sir? This new rope . . . "

"It's gotta be new rope!" The old man bent over, not touching the knot. "Yeah," he said grudgingly. "I guess. And you take this platform contraption – " he struck the boards under the iron lightly with his scuffed boot. "One more o' the Cap's new ideas – " he snorted and the boy jumped a little. "Useta be tough, man. None o' this soft psychology stuff. Carried it up right, right up there. We done it right then, but now – " the old man glared with a fierce brilliance at the other, his chin bristling over the mass of iron as the crest of Sun Rock emerged out of the mass of the island beyond the wide water. The boy turned frantically, slid between

42

the stiff pillars of people; not stopping until he felt his mother's arm about his shoulder.

He stood, panting a little. He said nothing and she did not ask. The peak of Sun Rock grew above the people's heads and the boy understood that they were approaching much closer to the highest point of the island than they ever did in their family boat-picnics. He looked to his father, but his head was high, eyes distant as if he saw nothing. The Capitular's voice was saying, "We hope you had a nice exploration tour, Joey. We were just beginning to wonder where you might be." His Highest was not looking at him as he spoke, but rather at what seemed to the boy was a watch one of the Lesser Capitulars was holding before him. Everyone stood silent, grim as if they had never smiled. The Capitular's face was the only friendly one; and suddenly the boy stepped forward.

"Sir, Your Highest, I saw Miss Grierson. But she didn't – look at me. At school we always played in the sand, Eric and me, and she – is something – " The Capitular, still smiling, threw a swift glance at the sky and stood up. The cantors began, their sound lifting unintelligibly into the warm morning, united, plaintive, strangely harrowing. The boy turned sharply for his mother but the Capitular's soft hand was on his shoulder, his voice in his ear.

"Come, my boy. I want you to do one thing, something just for me. For this you were chosen yesterday when you drew the Lottery." The boy gazed wide-eyed at him. The Lottery was for the ride. He twisted, one glance finding his mother now standing. Her eyes were dilated and her face pulled out of shape, but she was nodding soundlessly to him. He could not but obey and he walked forward, the heavy hand now very tight on his shoulder, through the lane opening between the people, hearing the chant merge to words as the motors throbbed and died under his feet. And then over the cantors, the high voice of the Capitular lifting and they were standing before the riddled bulk of iron on its little platform, the people all about and sounding now also, the morning sun just visible over the high thrust of the Rock.

" – *the-evergoodness-of-the undying-and-golden* – " but the boy did not hear, his eyes shifting from the water where there was now no bronze railing to interrupt his view of the wedge of boats sitting like gulls along the edge of the Rock's shadow on the blue-black water. In the hesitance of silence the Capitular bent to the boy, voice now almost sorrowful.

"Joey, do exactly as I say. This is the handle." The thick fingers pointed to a lever on a raised panel. "When I nod my head at you, pull it back. Just one little pull. It is very easy. But don't," the fingers closed on the boy's hand lifting, "don't touch it till I nod. Exactly then. That's my fine boy. Now, watch me. Exactly. When I nod."

The mesmerizing smile on the broad face, so close, held the boy watching the great arms lift as they did each week in the ambo, the sound of the cantors rising, rising to the top of comprehension and the world flaming with their incredible sound as the boy had never heard it in the rood-loft. He stood erect, swaying slightly to the sway of the people. Then the Capitular bowed to him, his hand found the handle and, standing all alone, facing the water now and the sun flush in his eyes over the peak of the Rock, he pulled.

The sound of the cantors was now the sound of all the people, swaying beyond the water's lift of the Yacht. The boy was the only one who saw the little platform stir and tilt at his feet and the iron slide from the deck like a living thing. Amazed, he stepped to the edge. The splattered circles of its falling fled away from the very apex of the Rock's shadow on the water and he saw the mass of it waver down into blackness and the white rope snake along the waterline, his eyes following, and seeing suddenly, beyond the people tight to the rail, the rope ending in a white form falling from the Yacht in one smooth motion. The form hesitated, flat, spread-eagled on the water like a great headed т crossed with a golden-and-crimson slash, before it smudged, then vanished in the black water. The boy stood, staring, remembering only the gaping hole in the mask-like face.

Under the sound of the people floating over the water, the old man was leaning over the railing, cursing softly. " – goddam motor block – so goddam many holes, gurgling to hear it above the chant! In the old days we used millstones. Clean, sure. Damn new-fangled stuff – "

The boy's fingers dug through his mother's thin black dress as she crouched down, clutching him to her.

"Mommie – Mommie – "

"Hush," said his mother. She shuddered in the sunlight. "Hush. Just hush."

There's a Muddy Road

"Why don't you take your shirt off too," Mary said, and laughed. That nervous little spasm of a laugh again. "I've never seen a naked man who didn't have a beard."

"I bet."

But she ignored his tone. "That wasn't so bad, now was it," she said. Her slender hand seemed to be curling around, among the red hair of his thigh. If he hadn't been staring at it, sitting knees up and forehead against his propped-up fists – Rodin's thinker no less, no, wrong position – he wouldn't have known she was touching him. Compulsive talker.

"No."

She laughed far too loudly for the empty room. Her tent dress loose around her, that she hadn't taken off and he didn't want her to take off now. He was feeling absolutely nothing at all. He found he could even look at her, down directly into her brown eyes in her unrecognizable up-side-down face and not even blink. "It takes time, we've both been married too long," she said.

A child called outside again.

"And besides, you always want something more, of course."

"More!" his snort exploded in his nose.

"I'd say this was barely a start," she said, laughing. That husband of hers she no longer loved flapping around playing word games, straggle-haired in blue jeans at the university, over thirty and on an eternal scholarship or assistantship or whatever it was the government kept forking over in tax money so he wouldn't have to finish his degree and get to work if he could find any, fuddling around with words, his care-for-nothing-but-love attitude was carved into her every laugh and sentence. He was even called 'Harry'.

"How'd you dare get married?" he had asked her once. "With names like you've got."

"They sang a song at the wedding, 'Mary and Harry will reach Tipperary.' The names were real fun, maybe that's why I married him when I was looking for a husband."

"Huh."

"My daddy said I was on my own, he wouldn't send me to school and the easiest way seemed to get married. I was a child then. He loves me too, and he's always been good to me."

"In his own way of course."

"Better than you in yours."

"Who started this?"

He realized he had said perhaps that last aloud. Perhaps all of it had been out loud, and he didn't care about that either because they'd been round and round with themselves on that so many times; it was all they ever had to do together with her twenty minute coffees or hour lunches, talk, though sometimes it was really laughing fun and the days and sometimes weeks when he knew there wasn't a chance he would see her, talking was the last thing he thought of doing with her. Sometimes there grew these great stupid plans of some night together in some luxury hotel in some city where no one knew him and not one other soul in the whole world would ever know about it to be bothered, simply one complete thoughtless perfect night, one '*Wow, outa sight!*' as his daughter would say, and that was it, exactly, that would wipe out the whole mess once and for all clean so he and she too would forget what she kept insisting she felt for him: love.

"It might have been okay, eventually," he had said. "We could have been friends and had our good laughs at lunch and maybe you could have got me to where I'd been willing to have as they say 'an affair' with you. When you first showed up I even thought about that. Any man always thinks that about any new girl that looks like something walking past and he sees her, nothing much personal about it, and he thinks the girl's young and has any number of chances and won't do it anyways so what the heck it's something to fiddle around with when houses aren't moving. You hear the guys."

46

"And that's what you thought of me."

"A passing thought, they go by all the time."

"Like your salesmen?"

"Look, I don't kiss women, or just accidently rub past them. I don't have 'affairs'. This whole now thing, it's not so new anyway, makes me sick because there's never anything to it but mess and more mess. Believe me, I've seen enough. I don't believe in living like that. I'm honest, I believe a man should love his wife for life and live with her and with his children. He's got to provide for them, why do you think I'm still in business? If it wasn't for them you think I wouldn't have cashed it all in long ago and done what I've always wanted? I could have too if I just said like your lovely Daddy, 'It's your life, you're on your own.' I'd be a doctor right now, don't you worry."

"You can't love me, and Alice and your children too?"

Mary was still lying stretched out beside him. Her very short unbelted dress as if flung on the gold rug, her right leg bent so that foot touched her ankle. Her legs were the best part of her, he had seen that the first time she walked in before he looked up and saw he knew her face. He remembered legs better than faces. The fast, lop-sided grins of men whose glance bushed past his, knowing, down to skirt lengths shamed him, but he was always looking there anyway before he became aware and deliberately looked away. She lay with her face upside-down to him and steadily looking up out of her dark eyes, which were the other good part of her, with her hair once you thought of it. Her body was too thin, her nose a bad turn and her complexion erratic. For the men an affair meant somebody stacked, some liberated thing on pills that didn't give a damn tomorrow. No part-time office help with a seven year old daughter and a bad teenage marriage, no matter what the legs.

He couldn't remember, had they said a word since he took off his shirt? He had taken it off. He was trying to think of something but he somehow felt nothing at all inside him; nothing, just an empty sack all over which could feel the coolness of the vacant house. Beyond the curtains behind him the sun would be baking the pavement. Several children called there.

"I don't like to leave the scene of a defeat," she said.

She reached up and tried to pull him down but her very words, straight out of her stupid Freud Bible or Reich or whatever she was always reading – if they weren't from there they sure sounded

47

like it – stung him and he pulled away. He put his hand against her shoulder, stood up and reached for his clothes crumpled against the drapes.

"This house is on multiple listing," he said out loud. It was only three seventeen; he couldn't believe so little time had passed and he had told Mrs. Rostok he was on a call the rest of the afternoon. Yeah.

"What happened if some salesman walked in?"

"I'd forgotten to unlatch the door, I was in the basement with my customer, you, and didn't hear the bell for a while. So."

"I like being your customer."

"You're not."

"Even just in case, and you had it all figured out?"

"Yeah."

"At last, a plan."

"Yeah." He was buttoning his shirt but he did not feel nonchalant. Had he ever? Maybe that was a lot of what had been wrong. He had felt just nothing, almost as if he had decided deliberately, a plan today, yes, and then the kids shouting beyond the drapes, rattling their wagons over the pavement of the bay and once earlier when he looked out the kitchen window a teenager who should have a job for the summer was leaning on the fence across the alley, studying his gleaming Buick. He should have parked in front, what salesman took a customer in from the alley? What had he been thinking of?

"Where's the bathroom?" She was up, already walking towards the hall.

"Straight ahead. There's one off the master bedroom too."

He observed himself in the bat-winged mirror; adjusting his tie. Exactly like in the narrow one at home, not a wrinkle, not a mark. Absolutely nothing. He settled his coat straight as he heard the water pipes singing. She had left the bathroom door open so he had seen the bend of her knees, and he stayed in the bedroom a moment. Its window also faced the alley; the kid wasn't leaning there now. All high back fences around the curve like pens at the stockyard. Her shadow shifted across a corner of the hall, and he went.

"I wouldn't buy this house, it's kitschy suburbia."

"You couldn't afford it, nobody can, they want far too much and think leaving the drapes will fool a stupid buyer."

"How convenient." She was standing at the steps of the back

48

entrance, looking across dining and living room to the drapes. "They're gaudy."

He was putting on his shoes he had left at the door. "They want thirty-seven five."

She laughed. "It'd be better in a tent."

Her laugh was no happy sound and because their best times had always been exactly such triggering back and forth and hounding down of double entendres, the last thing he wanted was to pick that up. And it was only three seventeen. Twenty-three now.

In the Buick she said, "Would you drive round the front?"

"Huh?"

"I'd like to see it from the front."

"I can give you the address too but the pho – "

"No, I don't want . . . " she interrupted and stopped as quickly. For an instant he almost felt pity. "Just see it."

He shrugged, backed all the way out to the street, then forward around and slightly into the bay and stopped. The children, three girls and a spindly boy, stared around, ready to scatter from hopscotch. "The mauve front with the empty planter and yellow-brick fireplace. That means it's four years old and next year it'd have to be new 'old brick' which style has already reached B.C. from California."

She said nothing and so he backed up and drove down the street. Through one grey-roofed Edmonton suburb and then another, his mind registering out of the corner of his eye the price of any house by size and exterior, out to the arterial street. The house market wasn't this year what it had been last, though still good; he should have cashed out three years ago. Every year helped, and got a little harder too. The radio was murmuring; he turned into a service station he had never used before on the highway now and bought four dollars worth of gas and three bottles of Pepsi because he saw the machine and felt suddenly thirsty. He got the attendant to clean the windshield again, properly, and then they were on the Calgary Trail. He kept just two miles under the speed limit, pushing down immediately when the signs were readable. From the radio came the echoed picking of electric guitars, that was, yes, The Sounds of – "Hello darkness my old. . . . " He turned it up.

He had first heard that the Friday evening he had promised to take Alice to see *The Graduate:* 'It tells you everything about today's generation,' which wasn't why the office was talking about it. That same afternoon Mary had come in with her last sheaf of letters because Mrs. Rostok was over having her baby and would be back Monday, and he watched her body move and her legs disappear thinking nonchalantly as he had more than a few times in those three weeks, 'It would be nice having you here all the time, every way girlie,' and then suddenly she was standing there again and he looked up to her face and saw she was crying. He had sense enough to get up and close the door.

"Sit down," he said. "What's wrong?"

He hated having women cry. That was one thing Mrs. Rostok never did, among others, like getting whistles just walking through the office. Mary's shoulder bag had slipped and when she was seated she reached for it; he thought she was getting something to blow her nose, but she unearthed her pocketbook and from the inner compartment behind some bills took a small blue paper. Despite her continued crying her slim hands moved efficiently as they always did. She held the paper to him without looking up. It was just a scrawled note he had placed with the first letters she had done for him: "You're one girl from Office Overload that can type *and* spell. I *like* that." He looked down at the white part of her hair. Her pocketbook?

The radio sounds were humming, echoing on and he managed another long swallow of Pepsi. Once he heard a certain song repeated when he was in a certain mood, he could not hear the song again without the same feeling rising to him. He had first become aware of his strange retention of sound and feeling the summer he finished high school and finally got a job pouring concrete that might make him enough to get to get to university. The crew was completely refugee, no one except the foreman could speak a word of English to him and all week he shovelled gravel for sidewalks into that scrapping mixer to the unintelligible shouting of those men in a small town out on the burning prairie and they slept in tents behind the town workshop where a generator thumped until no more electricity was needed and when it cut out in the middle of the night he always woke startled into the silence and with the snores of the muttering men he felt the terrible loneliness of that song drive into him which he heard every day sitting with them at the counter in the town's one Chinese cafe and the radio blaring always this one song. The tune wasn't actually that sad: it was hearing it there, again and again, as if the one station that could be reached had only one record.

The guitars clanged out on " . . . silence . . . " and he cut it off just before the announcer screeched. He knew suddenly he could not remember that song. Twenty-four years. That was impossible. it had been sung by Elton Britt. Elton Britt singing . . . he couldn't remember. There was only this haunting sadness he had first heard that night in that almost unbearable movie. Poor Elton driven under, wiped away.

He slowed, turned right towards the river. The road was gravel, potted with water. He slowed even more; he was just getting mud on the car. Mary was talking. He became aware of that as he looped his empty bottle over into the ditch. He'd heard it before, there was probably nothing she had to say he hadn't heard before.

" . . . and we'd moved there just that spring when you came home from graduating from Alberta and their star basketball player too and the principal had you talk to the whole school assembly. He was so proud, smiling, and I was ten then in grade four, without a single friend. Daddy had moved us there practically the end of the year. You talked up there so tall and confident and that's when I started to love you."

He had admitted to her once, when she really pushed him, that he liked to remember her saying that. "Okay, I'll be honest with you. Knowing you've said that gives me confidence. It helps me when I feel in a corner." But he could not understand it: he could not believe a woman could have loved him all those years, to the very summer twenty, and he not know a single thing of it, hardly even have heard her name for eighteen. Glimpses he'd never known about when he visited his parents, far away, down streets. How could that be love? If only one person knew about it and never so much as made a plan to say a word until a pure job accident pushed in? Eighteen years, with jobs and marriages and kids all thrown into the mixer by both of them and all of a sudden she pulls out this stupid little note and cries for love. It sure shafted friendship. Or anything.

"I can't think of what baloney I said there."

"It wasn't so bad. You were going to work awhile and go back to school, just the usual thing about working and doing your best."

"So why in the world?"

"You need a reason?"

"Oh sure," and that was believable about her, her frankness, but he couldn't believe what she told him. "I can't stand this mad running around. It's never anything but a mess, a hopeless mess believe me and I've never done it, not that I didn't have the chances."

"I know that."

"Okay, and when I first saw you I thought, 'Well, like usual the one with the best – figure is married, but I think something like that of any girl, I can't be a saint and when I found out who you were I remembered you from back home, of course, and I thought we could be friends and was going to invite you over or something with Harry – "

"And I spoiled it?"

"Yeah."

"Then why didn't you leave me alone? After that? I said my bit and you didn't believe me. I'd been holding that so many years and when I worked for you it was – I knew for certain why I had wanted to love you and did and do, more than ever – why do you keep calling up and we have lunch and coffee together and getting me to talk? Why don't you leave me alone?"

"I like to hear you talk. I like being friendly. You're from my home town and I like you."

She was staring at him; he could see that as he looked ahead and avoided a puddle; took the car over a rise and slowly down into the valley. It wasn't the river yet, just a creek crossed by a narrow bridge; a track led into the summer-green poplars beyond it on the left.

"Okay," he said, "that's not all. I've said it before, you give me confidence. And," he hesitated, then said fast, "when you're not around I think of all kinds of things we could do together, some place alone but when we're together I don't want to. You just don't do anything like that to me, as you know now, not even . . . " he was far enough into some lie, he didn't know exactly which and it certainly wasn't all lie either, to stop. He turned the car down into the crooked track. It was even muddier than the gravel, the car bounced violently and then he stopped. Out of sight from the road anyway, under the trees.

"You don't know anything about love."

"Have it your way. Like always." He got out, carefully onto the

52

grass, into the cool air that smelled of rain still. What sky he could see was absolutely blue; not a puff of cloud.

She was walking away on the muddy trail toward the sound of the creek. He followed on the grass, watching the bare brown feet lift, sink gently into the black mud. Her ankles seemed a little thicker than he remembered them but her tanned legs without stockings were fantastic.

"You think it's some fantastic club that will clout you, knock you silly and forget everything, jab you in the groin. That's all. Have you ever loved anyone, have you ever loved Alice, have you?"

"I love Alice."

"I know she's very beautiful, much more attractive than I but she's not happy and you aren't. I'd never said a word to you if I hadn't felt you were desperately unhappy. Why do you think I said nothing for so long? You were getting all those calls from her, and the children too, then, and I could hear you holding down your anger and frustration and you were so cruel to them, and that isn't like you, I couldn't stand it. You were so terrible on the phone, you couldn't love her. You never talk as if you do."

"You can tell that, just like that."

"Yes."

"You should talk."

"I don't love Harry any more and I've told him. He knows, and he still loves me and has made me very happy at times, but we're frank with each other. We talk through what is and what isn't. What do you and Alice tell each other? How much is in the bank? You sound as if you've never talked to her."

"Sure, you can tell that too."

"That's the trouble, I can. You never deny what I say and – "

"Some things between man and wife you don't talk about to anybody."

" – and you keep on with your boy's dream of being a man of great knowledge and healing some day when you do perfectly good things like selling houses, honestly, and people need salesmen who sell houses honestly as much as they need doctors. And that's something that's good about you too," she added sadly, sitting down without a glance. "You keep thinking you want to do it."

They were at the creek, she sitting sideways a little above the mud of its bank. The water was swollen a glossy brown with rain and whorled in the sun turning past them, out from under willows against the high clay it had sheered off at their right, held straight for fifty yards and then bent sharp out of sight to the left. The willows just below them were almost completely submerged. As she said nothing he saw three boys appear out of the bushes on the left and run down the incline to the creek. One had a knapsack, another an air rifle; they seemed the age of his oldest son. They did not look up; laughing and pushing they walked right into the water spinning from its turn as if it wasn't there, as if they had already taken off their shoes and clothes. The now generation all right, his daughter walking into the lake with jeans on just like that, ducking around and screeching with her friends 'Wow – Wild!,' water running off them and sticking their tee shirts to their bra-less chests it was obscene and answering nothing to his yell but 'Oh shut dad!' But the current made these boys aware, staggering them nearly to their waists while they laughed, still grabbing each other and pushing until suddenly the kid without the knapsack or rifle slipped, vanished into a blaze of light off the brown water, and in an instant his head resurfaced against the bank, sputtering. His two friends seemed to go beserk with laughter, staggering about in delirious imitation, then they were all three dragging themselves up the slimy groove in the opposite bank, laughing, leaping to watch the water squitch out of their shoes, slipping down the groove again to the edge of the creek and grabbing legs and roots and willows to clamber up somehow. Finally they were all up on the level and shrieking they ran off, directly through the puddles on the path, scattering them like spray as they disappeared.

"That kid really soaked his gaunchees," he said. "That would have been something, if he's disappeared and I'd have had to help fish him out."

She should have caught up something smart, like how would he have explained his muddy pants to Alice, but she was staring up the trail where they had gone.

"I've had enough," she said, "you and your absolutely spotless Buick."

"You've only had one ride in it."

"That's enough. There are other men. I'm going to make myself beautiful."

"How'll you do that?" But she refused even that tinge of nastiness. "You've said that a few times before too."

"It's really enough now. You'll never make up your mind, you just want everything and neat and clean too. I've loved you very much and you won't do anything about it. You think it would be nothing but a mess if we were together and that I couldn't make you happier than Alice. I know I could and she'd be happier too, but you won't believe me. I've made Harry happy and I don't love him, the only thing that makes him unhappy now is you. Knowing I'm always thinking about you and you such a dog."

"Dog?"

"It's his word for your kind."

"I'm a 'kind'?"

"To him yes, not to me. And you haven't even told Alice I exist."

"She knows you took over when Mrs. . . . . " it was too inane and he stopped.

"Two years." She was tossing tiny stones into the spinning creek, one by one. "I know that if we could sleep beside each other, peacefully and happily, it would be very beautiful. Even when I was a girl I always thought there had to be a God for how else could I explain love and the strange pull of it in such a strange place in my body?"

"That's just sex."

"Love has everything to do with your body. And with everything else you are too."

"Mary," he said suddenly, "I always thought that the most beautiful, the most divine thing was that somewhere among all the world's billions of people there was one woman, and one only, who was my true love. I believe that."

She said nothing. Her long fingers kept on finding stones beside her muddy feet.

"I'm going to leave him," she said. "I don't know when, maybe soon. He's a lovely father, he'll take better care of Ruthie than I, and we've been really happy together. The happier a man and a woman have been the sooner they separate once the happiness is gone."

"You're just saying that. They'd work at it all the harder."

"They know too well what's missing, and they can't take it."

"That's too easy," he said. "I don't believe it. No. I can't."

Did Jesus Ever Laugh?

Around this apartment at least they haven't stuck in trees for birds to sit on and try to sing. Just bushes to keep you off the patch of grass too small for a gopher and then up blank like a north end coulee in fall, twenty stories cement straight up and down, maybe seventeen apartments on each, say around twelve or thirteen hundred in all; you know, a grey slab box with metal windows. In twelve or thirteen hundred, a place like this, there should be one. One at least. You'd think so, wouldn't you, but you can't count on it; I've tried a few. Football and hockey games aren't worth the snot you blow waiting and the late movie's absolutely blank. Nothing. There's too much of this people coming out now trying to jack themselves down after some man's north end been flipping through the sheets. It's just nothing like it was.

You'd think a place the size of Edmonton (over four hundred thousand friendly people says the sign on the Calgary Trail), it's amazing with that number of people and all that preaching flushing through their heads how few there really are in the whole city. At least the few I've seen, and I spend my time looking. I'm never not looking and I know; there are but few. Bars and nightclubs have always been like you know, hopeless. The biggest encouragement I ever had about Edmonton was I found two within four feet of each other at the Willingman Brothers Evangelistic Revival Incorporated last year when they come out at the Gardens. In broad daylight! By the time I could move they had both disappeared and I nearly lost them, both. They say Billy Graham could be coming next fall, but it's probably too much to pray for.

So that's why I was on apartment blocks now, in broad daylight. Waiting actually isn't too bad there sometimes, with the clouds down and November wind prying in where the liner's torn away on the old Lincoln's doors. It's a beautiful car yet, better every year. I can see it black, from here. I work it over with hard wax at least once a week, you know really sweat it with elbow grease like I always did. All the soft parts in it are about gone and I've got these nice hard boards shoved under the seat covers where I sit. On days like that I can sit, watching and waiting, wherever I've parked and I'll get numb slowly till there's no feeling in me at all and I'm just sunk down, eyes along the bright black edge of the hood, watching. Not feeling a thing, just eyes, waiting.

But this fall's been bad; the summer was cold and rainy but now in October the sun shines as if it's gone mad and Edmonton was prairie. The leaves come gliding off the trees and it's warm and people walking around without coats. It gets so you – I – can't sit at all; all of a sudden I have to get out even when I have a good parking space and the meter doesn't have to get fed. I just have to get out, walk around in the sunshine if you can imagine that, I have to rub behind my knees where the edge of the board cuts. It's terrible; I stand there feeling my blood move. The warm air washing over my face. It's so bad then I even forget the words.

But today, no sunshine. I could sit in the car easy just off the corner where this poured slab was sticking up, holding the concrete clouds. A few dozen had gone by, in and out, but they were no good. One glance will always tell me, I never need more. You're watching and waiting; it seems like all my life now I've spent like this, watching and waiting and there always being so few, so few, for weeks it's hanging in your mind there aren't any left anywhere in the world and then it happens like it always has who knows how it's almost past before you suddenly know and you wonder how many you maybe missed just like that because you were hopeless even while you're sitting up, slowly, careful, feeling it, letting it soak into you again as you're looking and moving, always like the first time at that circus and dead-white up high against the canvas the white leg starts out, feeling slowly along something you can't see but it must be there while the drum rolls and you tighten, slowly, and then so sudden you haven't seen the move she's standing complete, alone, white arms crossed out, standing up there above everything on nothing. Though you know there has to be a wire. I was on the sidewalk, standing, and walking then. Not fast, just enough to stay behind, feeling the tightness work me like a beautiful dull ache towards the grey block, under the grey porch, and the tune was there, the words and tune too right there as if I was soaked with it,

> *Leave the dance with me sweet Sally,*
> *Come with me just*

walking just fast enough to stay behind because a woman with a heavy bag of groceries will not, of course, walk very fast.

With only one bag the outer door was no trouble; she swung that easily and I was slowing down so I wouldn't come up and show I had no key by not offering to open the inner one (wear a tie and always move calm, that's all) but it was all fine, of course, just fine as it always is if you've been able to wait long enough: a man all in black pushed out that minute and held the door, she didn't have to bother with a key. I went in fast and caught the door as it started shut after her. I nodded but the man was past and didn't even grunt; he went past without a look at his best deed for the day. When I see him again, I'll thank him.

Two steps up to three closed elevator doors; there was a rubber rug on the floor, and the little lobby off the front door had three bile-green couches and a coffee table with a comic book ripped like some kids had been tearing their hair out there. A blown-up kodachrome saved wallpaper on one wall. Mountain lakes! I can't stand them. Where we waited for the elevator was a trough of dark broad plants with flowers stuck in sandpails. The flowers were big as my fist and cold, just beautiful.

The middle elevator thumped and five people came out, one a woman with a weiner-dog on a string and two girls. Their stockings were mottled white so their legs looked like dead birch sticking in a puddle, but the rest of them – ugh – they were ugly, so smooth and round-faced with long straight hair the way you see them now wherever you look in the world. And tight skirts so short when they sit they'd show to the crotch, their boobs sticking out, it was obscene,

O look it's grey out.
I said bring your coat.
This lipstick doesn't match it.
O look it's so grey.
I said bring your coat.

But my ear-rings . . . .
their stick legs tapping along the rubber rug, twitching each band-
age of a skirt.

She had pushed her floor and I leaned over the panel to push
the same one, just in case she was looking. But she wasn't, of
course. Why should anybody look at me? They never do, especially in elevators where there are more than two people; even
when there are only two. People in cities don't look at each other;
their glances slide over, like the man standing beside me with a
face as if he'd slept maybe two minutes in some can last night and
nicotine all over his cigarette fingers, letting the smoke curl at me.
That's just the way it is, always, somebody's cancer poking at your
face, you can count on it like the sun rising

. . . with me just once more.
Follow me tonight, we'll take the boat from shore.
I will keep you warm, sweet Sally,
In your dan

the door was open and she going, I almost hummed it away. But
of course I was moving (even if I'd lost my arm in the door)
following like a gentleman, and turned left as she turned right, the
hall carpet under my feet and one glance at a door number as she
walked down the lighted hall – 1808 – and wheeling after her, only
three strides behind when she stopped by a door, fumbling in her
shoulder purse, and just beside her as the top of the grocery bag
split from her tilt and movement, split so I can stick out my hand
for the box of Tide sliding out, grab the whole grocery bag, like a
gentleman, just perfect, it is absolutely just perfect.

"Oh – " then softer, "oh – thanks, that – yes, thank you," reaching.

I might as well hold it now, you open up.

"Oh, yes, of course," the key is out as she hesitates, "it usually,"
and in the lock, "I should have put it down," turning, "but usually
I usually manage," the door clicks and she looks up from its little
movement, her hands coming up to take the bag and she'd have
touched my hands doing it if I hadn't jerked away, my shoulder
swinging the door in – don't for god's sake don't not yet – so I can
hardly get my mouth open,

I – I m-might as well – as well c-carry it in . . .

Her glance flickers up at me in the dim hall light and I step in

60

fast – don't give her a chance not a chance – 1815 – and in the little hall with the usual white plaster walls and the kitchen straight ahead my heart slows, settling back even as I hesitate with my back to her still somewhere in the doorway, or maybe the hall,

Where would you like it, please?
like a gentleman delivery boy. The hesitation is all I need, just a little pause you see, little things always will happen but you cut through them with calm direct action and they're no problem. Then just take a deep breath and away you go.

"Anywhere I – on the kitchen counter – my mother-in-law, you needn't – "

No trouble at all, I might as well, and among the dirty dishes I thrust the bag, I might as well, careful with two egg-marked plates, turning to her in perfect calm and look. Now. The big move left. It's starting to roll and a man in black goes past in the hall behind her but doesn't so much as glance, it's starting as I start to the door. Her face loosens like she pulled a cord. She shifts sort of sideways, smile and words start slow, then burst as she opens just a little in relief,

"That was – oh, very kind, of you, I was downstairs washing and the detergent ran out so I hopped down to the grocery while my mother-in-law was. . . . " – ooo lady you've got a long way to go – I'm hearing her, I guess, where she stands aside against the coat closet in the grey apartment hall, talking, shifting as I move so there's thirty inches between us, steady, as I reach for the door and she is back between the kitchen's dutch doors, separating them, the light (a momentary break of sunshine outside?) from the window like bullets spraying from her black solid lovely shape as I turn from closing the door and slipping up the door chain without so much as a small rattle, can lean back then against that closed door; and look. The song really rolling now

> . . . *Sally*
> *In your dancing gown,*
> *Warm as the tropic sea*
> *Far from the lights of t*

rolling so I have to wrench myself erect or right then and there I'll be already into the chorus!

She is making a sound; I don't hear quite and her face is in shadow as the light fades again, but her hands go slowly up to her throat, first one and then the other. I'm standing solid now, weight even on my two feet and everything back under control; I always have to watch that, when the first stage ends. Once after too long I got rolling so strong I – well, spilt milk.

Excuse me, I move to see the lashes on her eye. You talking to me? She's now against the kitchen counter and her hands drop. Just my right height for a woman, five foot six. Her voice, well, there've been better, but not bad. With other things, the voice is fringe benefit.

" . . . the – no idea who you are. I thanked you for your" her arm lifts a little; she has nice motion that way; "and now, go."

Of course not.

She hasn't a touch of make-up and her eyes dead grey, as they have to be. Not a speck of colour in her eyes. Her face going like stone, she turns, very nice, and walks past the table off the kitchen and around the partition into the living room and while she is still far enough away not to get hurt by something flying I put a bullet through the telephone. The silencer cost me but it's the best you can get; the shot is no louder than a kid falling on its head out of a highchair; the noise is the telephone flying apart on the bookshelf, what's left of it crashing to the hardwood. The bell clangs as it hits, something sizzles

We are all alone, sweet

but I can cut that one easy. Her move rushed me a little and I'm already in the second verse. That's not so good.

You shouldn't of made me do that. Take this out so quick. I put it away. Rushing don't help a thing.

Her back is like you pulled a lever and turned her to rock, half-tilted against the bookshelf. After a while her little finger starts to jerk back and forth a little on the spine of a book lying there; it looks like a Bible, lying with bits of black telephone on its black cover.

Where's Mother-in-law?

Her finger stops; after a while she whispers, not turning, "Mother-in-law?"

Yeah. When we come in. Where's she?

"She – she lives in Vauxhall, three hundred miles – "

That's okay, I was born in Alberta, I know enough about

62

Vauxhall. All right. Would you kindly show me around, you know.

"Show you. . . . "

Just take it easy, around the apartment I mean, that's all.

She wheels so fast I think she's ready for something and look up from her ankles quick, but she's just on the edge of crying. That's no good at all; is she the wrong

"Please, oh please, for the love of – "

Don't do that! and she stops very fast. You know how I can't hold my hand with a voice like that and I have to talk fast. Just don't do that, talk like that. Just business, like you wanted to sell, okay, and I was buying? Now show me the apartment.

She's looking at me and her face hardens again – I knew it, she's the cream the real solid kind who pick it up fast – slowly hardens out of her other expression. She walks ahead of me, voice stripped like she's selling the place,

"You – saw the kitchen, dining area, living room. This is the hall closet."

That's handy, right by the door. I'm standing back a bit, look-ing forward mostly to be polite; hall closets don't do much for me.

"Each apartment has them there" – atta girl edge in your voice edge – "and this is the storage area, small but conven . . . "she's got the door open and with a twist before I start to see it she's half inside and I've got to grab her, get both my hands out and actually grab her! Yank her before she's inside and the door slammed behind her and who knows what they've got in

all alone, sweet Sally,
Far from the dance on shore,
Where your lovers wait to

that far into the second verse and not ten minutes with her. She's rushing me, that's all I can say, she's a good one, the best maybe but she's rushing me and I can't say anything at all when I break myself out of it and get my face and hands more or less calmed down again (sometimes I've never had to use my hands at all, you know that) and she's staring at me from where she's spread against the dim wall in the hallway, staring up till I can finally get my face quiet and my hands down. My jaw unlocked.

It's that door, that one. Don't you make one move.

It was her fault, that TV trick with the storage room, and she knows it. I have the one closed bedroom door open without taking my eyes off her, bent back, hands still spread where she caught herself, back against the wall. The shades are drawn, it's even nicer dark in there, but I've got to see sharp now so I reach in with my left hand and flick on the light. An instant is enough; a grey bun of hair on the bed facing the other way and a quilt over the shoulders. The quilt helps. There's hardly a twitch and it's done in a flick, no different from putting two into the dummy out on the range so fast and tight the sergeant can't yell a thing because if he's got two bits to his name he can cover both holes. The song and tune holding it right on

> lovers wait to hold you close once more.
> But you'll dance again sweet Sally,
> As you glide on down,
> Down, down in the sea far

though I'm still a little mad she pushed me so fast. It's not really right and when I think about it later it'll be such a waste, so fast now. You really should have time to think about it all, step by step. Appreciate. Well – I've put it away, and my hands are free again. The door's shut.

Into the living room, you can sit on a chair, okay?

I knew she was right. She gets herself straightened up, it takes time but she does and she walks quite steadily into the living room and makes it fine to the armchair beside the bookshelf. The couch across the room for me. Just fine. Beautiful in fact.

You understand of course it's never happened this fast before, so much and so fast. I would never have dreamed to find anyone who could handle it the way she does, that would have been out of the question to imagine seeing I had such terrible waits even finding anyone. Oh, the waiting I've done, sitting, my body going dead sitting, or sometimes walking a little, waiting outside all those buildings in a place the size of Edmonton, four hundred thousand friendly souls and how can it be I couldn't, didn't find anyone, no one after you, and you – ah-h-h – just sitting here across from her with her slim legs decently together and skirt over her knees even when everything has exploded as it were in her usual life, to sit there and face me again with a dark solid face like rock and I don't have to begin anything. She will keep facing me I know without a word and her face set until I'm good and ready to start. When I'm ready.

There is, of course, no reason in the world why a human being should laugh.

I stop there like usual; I'm so sure now I don't have to bother at all timing it, that she'll butt in. She sits, her arms down along her thighs but she is not slumped. She does not blink and I am sitting right where her eyes seem to meet, although they don't seem quite to see me. She's alive and perfectly inert the way one can only dream and even then knowing you'll wake up before you can taste it all but there's no waking here, not now

Down, down in the sea
Far from the lights of town, Michael row

but that's trouble, the last verse starts like the chorus and if I don't watch that – you remember don't you – I'll be on in the chorus at last before the last verse because the first words are the same, and then it's been wasted all! All! But now I sense it of course right away, the second word in the last verse is 'weep' and I pull up. With someone like this I can probably keep this going – well I can try again can't I – the complete song, every verse, she looking like she is, so I cut the song and continue. At my leisure.

The problem with laughing is it makes you forget. You relax and the bad you've done you begin to forget it. Right away. That's wrong, you see. Don't you. You shouldn't just be able to forget about what you've done wrong. You should have it right there in front of your thinking all the time, know every wrinkle of it. Not wash it away with a laugh or a grin or a big-laugh and slap on the back. You gotta keep it in front of you all the time and that's the biggest thing that's wrong with laughing because it washes it out, you relax and it's gone, right out of sight and out of mind and that shouldn't happen like that outa sight and outa mind which is where laughing gets you because people should just hafta see and keep on seeing and staring right in the face every bit of everything and they've done ever done. . . .

Her expression has changed, and it's just as well because it breaks up my talk. Maybe she said something? I know, I was stumbling already, repeating myself. That's another thing that usually happens when it's so long. I repeat and then I'm going in circles. I know that, you don't have to – it's hard to stop, like some other things, unless you get help and here again she's got it. Just the look is enough and I can get stopped. No problem; start again.

You know these men nowadays call themselves theologians and call others to a new morality and call God dead? No doubt you've heard all about that, you can't get away from it hardly unless you plug yourself up, eyes, ears, nose, everything – well, God is dead for them, sure, because they've laughed him to death. There's just nothing left sacred and serious but somebody cuts it up laughing. Can you think of anything they don't laugh at now? I could give you ten minutes and you couldn't think of nothing, bright as I know you are. The Devil in the Snake got Eve to eat the apple by cracking a joke about God and the Devil's been laughing ever since. You laugh and you don't keep the proper things down no more – you get rid of them, right. The stuff's got to be kept down, down where it belongs and not laugh it away, and whatever you do you've got to be able to face it, square face to face and face it right out, and not once do you laugh it away easy. You do every bit you do dead sober, you live a godly, righteous and sober life like the Bible says, right. A righteous and sober life, facing everything you do without. . . .

She may have been saying something again. I can't be sure of course, because I was explaining to her, but she may have been saying something because I see now that her mouth is moving and it may have been moving and it may have been probably moving for some time. Her hand has definitely moved; she has the Bible in her hand now and is brushing the bits of black telephone off, holding it clutched in front of her with her eyes closed like sleep, but her lips move.

Right like the Bible says. I know you're a Bible reader, and I believe what the Bible says too. I don't always do right, I know that, and I've been punished, don't think I haven't, but I'm never getting punished because I didn't know and didn't care I was doing wrong. I'll know it before anybody else. The trouble with the world that walks past every day is they don't know they're doing wrong and they don't care if they did because they're so busy laughing it away. Everything's laughed at. People are always looking around, hoping to see something they shouldn't see, something to laugh. Women wear clothes – not you but there's plenty right in this building with you, you've seen them, showing things God never meant to be shown and people look and look and laugh to cover up the evil grinding in their heads when they look. Smiling everywhere, just notice it sometime. It isn't right and I've got the proof for it. You know the final proof?

I wait, like I always can afford and I know from this one I'll get response. But I'm so relaxed, and the verse comes

Michael weep for dear sweet Sally
Down in the deep blue sea,
Hang you head and cry down by the gallows tr

thanks heavenly God she's been saying something again, though I haven't heard it, and her staring mouth moving helps me cut across to her and hear her saying, aloud

" . . . ever done, what have I ever done to anybody that you – "

Heyhey now, I've got to jump in here fast. I can't have overestimated her, but dear God! Now that is no question for us sitting here like this. Don't do that, don't do that at all.

And she stopped, of course. She sits there motionless again, holding the Bible, her fingers dead white along the edges. The darkness has come in more from outside and someone I know is walking down the hall. You can hear him even with the thin rug there. This place was really built on the cheap, and maybe I should have figured that more before. I guess I did but I didn't think of all the possible implications of that, though by now you'd think I'd know better. Mistakes; I keep doing wrong and one of these – cut that!

You've got the proof right there, in your hand. The Bible. The Book of Jesus. You ever read that Jesus laughed?

She doesn't say a word that I can hear. Her eyes are wide, looking, her face rigid and her lips moving but I can't hear a word so I carry right on or I'll be through all that last verse and then there's nothing left but the chorus.

No. You never. You'll never read that we know right now, both of us, Jesus never done it. He healed the blind and wiped off the sores of lepers and threw out devils and whipped moneychangers and told Pharisees they were just so many sonsabitches and he gave the hungry food sometimes. But when did he ever laugh? Eh? You ever catch Jesus laughing? Nosir.

" . . . talking of Jesus after the unspeakable things you've . . . "
she goes on talking, her face still rigid like it's been cast forever but
her hand gesturing down the apartment hall.

The old woman now, right, and she went in sleep. She never
knew a thing of it. We should all pray for that. She could have
lived to ninety-five, here and in Vaux – the – the medicine, they
have, now, and her teeth falling out and not able to control herself
and you always wiping up her mess. Oh, I know, Jesus raised some
from the dead, about three the Bible says, and some relatives
thanked him for it but you never read nothing from the ones that
was raised, do you? Not a thank you, not from one of them. He
never done it for the dead ones, let me tell you, it was the living,
just some of them, nagging him. Anyway, if he did it for the dead,
why didn't he do it more? Tell me that. There must have been
plenty dead with Jesus walking the country and he just raised
three. Nosir. There's nothing to worry about the dead. They never
laugh. Not even when they come back.

I must have been talking a long time. My mouth feels dry and
she has pulled herself back in her chair, as if she were trying to
push back as far as she could. Has she been saying something?
Perhaps. Maybe that's why for a minute the sun coming in
through the slatted window, the big one in the living room where
we sit, my body coming back now a bit and relaxing on what once
was a good foam-rubber coach but now worn thin and thread-
bare, though it's really clean, I seem to have lost where I was.
Even the – no –

Down in the deep –
Hang your – head and – cry down by the gall

No, that's there okay. But it's so far gone. I must have been
wasting it somewhere, and she's talking too; I can hear her.

I've heard it all before, yeah, he raised three and loved them
all. So in all them hundreds of years since, how many you think he
killed?

That's everybody's mistake about Jesus. He had a lot more
things in his mouth than love. That's the forgotten Jesus. Like
hanging stones around your neck and into the sea with you, down
down, or calling a woman that isn't a Jew like him a dog, just like a
lot of other Jews do now, just walk down the pawn street and you'll

68

hear. Or that about the sheep and the goats. Everybody lined up, all the nations, great and small it says right here in your Bible, Matthew chapter 25, and the big finger coming out and the voice, 'You sheep right', and 'You goat left'. That's judgement, and sheep and goats sliding right and left without so much as a snicker anywhere. Dead sober, dead, and the goats knowing dead sure why they're going. They know why. Because compared to a sheep a goat's a LAUGHER

    Sheep   the range flat grey powdered rock dusted in hollows to grey chewed root   sheep-like clouds, white on grey-green, white in the streaky blue   the horizon so far and straight the hills turning on a shimmer of griddle heat   sheep like clouds, sheep whitish pancakes fuzzing grey in the heat, frying flat, speckled under the specks of hawks stuck on the blue for gophers   above hawks and sheep and flat grey to the horizon end in sky hang vultures, flat, sailing like dead ashes hooked on the heat over the impossible level of sage and stubble gnawed grey by sheep and gophers and the unending sun   soft at the flat edge of it, almost gentle but slowly hoisting itself higher and higher to burn over the gaunt woolly sheep panting against each other, sides thumping in the heat till their backs merge in the shimmer of flat earth sweating greyness and light under the ash of vultures endless turning turning   sheep. The goat standing in the one patch of shade   beside the sleeping-wagon   alone in a herd of sheep   no female to chase in a small surge through the flat backs and a momentary lunging elevation   a female of his kind   always erect already in whatever shade, on whatever elevation, a sweat-spot beside the wagon or any stone large enough for two hooves   head erect, horns curled back   chewing   standing and chewing endless under the ash   chewing with a twist to his mouth, head turning from the panting sheep smeared flat over the land   facing ahead, a twist in his mouth   the flat blazing earth flimmering   in heat

    . . . where's the girl?

    She stops what she has been saying to me; whatever it all was. Her mouth just stops and she is looking.

    "Excuse me?" she says finally. "Please!"

    Your girl? She at school now I guess? She just stares. Over there, the picture. I see everything. How old is she?

    "It was, just last, fall, before she started school, just last, we got

69

that picture. . . . " She's staring at me now and the expression on her face is changing again. She is looking at her wristwatch and her expression is changing as I watch, her fingers slowly kneading the smooth leather of the Bible.

In the dark northern lights come and go   washing out the stars in colour with their slow twitch   alone in a world bending flat backwards   the goat's white tail flickers   you can step off into stars   his black head nodding. He coughs.

" . . . finally dressed, it was such a hurry. And like I said when we finally got there, after all the fuss of the accident right in the underpass, it wouldn't have really caused any trouble if it hadn't happened right in the underpass, we almost cancelled everything, but Jake said it couldn't be helped, it wasn't his fault and Mama had come from Vauxhall to see her start school so why go through it all again but we were all so upset it came out stiff upset by the accident she's usually such a happy little girl the photographer tried everything and even got out his jack-in-the-box but she didn't want to laugh. He tried everything and Jake almost choked but she just couldn't seem. . . . "

down by the gallows

her mouth stops. And her face breaks. Breaks like when a hammer hits a dried-out clod of southern Alberta gumbo

     tree
     Michael weep for

She is screaming. Sitting perfectly motionless holding the Bible in front of her, staring at her wristwatch, screaming.

"God my God my God, that horrible song, stop it! STOP IT!"

I told you she was the right one. The song is in my head of course, I've of course never sung it out loud again and I wouldn't, you know that, even with her, but she knows. She's that kind

  dear sweet

she's on her feet, screaming, moving *her dancing* coming toward me, her hands set like claws *Drifting in the tide* too fast! It's too fast, she's coming too fast, reaching *the lights of town Michael row the* but it's too fast! I can't finish! I just can't jam it all in so
FA-A-A-A

The blanket from the shelf in the hall closet covers her easily.

70

Even the Bible lying there, splattered out. I shouldn't have counted on her that much. Depended so much. Sitting so still, talking so long and perfectly normal – weren't you talking about your life, all those growing up things, don't you remember? – I should have expected she'd break and got it finished. But it was so comfortable, at last. That was my mistake, I know, but we have to have time or it doesn't do any good. You taught me that, too. And this almost worked, you can't really say it didn't, till you had to spoil it but it worked – well, it's a minute to four – all afternoon? She was better than anyone, since. In a place the size of Edmonton, to find so few! But there's still the little girl. Is there?

I'm sitting erect on the window sill eighteen floors up. There's no balcony, this place is too cheap, and there's not even a screen but my head is very steady on heights so it is not dangerous at all. Though it has never been this high before. The black bridge, beautiful with black heavy steel, reaches over the valley, low water glinting here and there under the sodden clouds. Apartment blocks stick up all over but the black level line is the best thing about the best thing about the valley, a line straight across the green hollow, though now in late fall the leaves are finally gone there is mostly grey left. They are gone. The valley, the river, the road and the spidered trees, the sideway and the parking lot approach below. All variations on grey.

Four o'clock so it must be very close to time. The sun pretty well gone. A black spot of someone comes out from under the porch and cuts across the grey, passing behind my black Lincoln. I sit. She'll be coming soon. Has there been pounding on the door? I listen but then, how can you tell? The song hanging there, waiting, still waiting to be finished finally. Flat Vauxhall. Is someone pounding? Is there?

Or is it a knock? Ah-h-h-h-h

All on Their Knees

I

Down on one knee he thrust his arms under, groping for a grip. It was curled, head and arms balled round to belly and knees. He fought the blizzard's weight and that unyielding curl, sweat bursting from his pores. For a long moment he curled over, around it, fumbling and hugging at its iron cold as if in love, then he got his arms locked and heaved erect. He staggered; the world wheeled over under the gritted snow and, incredible wonder, balanced on the sleigh track, a hard sure line for his feet.

Gradually a shadow bunched in the streaking white and he was floundering beside the sleigh. He tipped it in, felt for the reins; the horses moved as he clambered up. He tugged his robe over it and hunched behind the dash, heart violent in his chest.

Turn-off, make the turn-off, there's nothing beyond. Head down and mitt over his mouth, he breathed deeply once and again, then he stood up. No bush alongside; he could not even see the horses' heads now; only their rumps, occasionally bellies, remained, dark and heaving. My god if the tracks are drifted too much and they miss – in the wind – something – he thrust back his hood and the blizzard awakened his numb face. Nothing. He forced his lips to a whistle, the thin sound swallowed as it left his mouth, but suddenly a wild bark, and Roarer was plunging beside the sleigh. He yelled, "Hey, hey! Get up there!" reaching down. The dog sprang at his mitt and vanished ahead.

The wind shifted to eddy and bush formed on the right. Once they turned, the blizzard's sweep was broken by poplar and spruce but the drifts were higher. The black was nearly finished. The reins told him this, and its momentary lag behind the bay in leaping at

73

each new snow-ridge. The timing staggered so badly that once the black's haunch jammed the sleigh an instant before it leaped, the sleigh struck the drift at an angle and he had to hurl himself flat against the tilt. Something struck him behind the knees then and he crumpled across the dash. Rein pressure gone, the horses almost floundered but he jerked erect, screaming, slapping and they plunged on. On the hard level between drifts, he shoved the shape away from his feet back under the robes.

Mutt's barking welcomed them to the homestead clearing and the wilder storm. He snapped the icicles off the horses' nostrils and left them spent in their stall. At the sleigh again, he got one leg in, heaved it against himself and staggered to the door. Its very rigidity calmed him; like a heap of firewood he propped it up on his knee to lift the latch.

Where in the – well – he hooked a table leg and dragged the table from the wall. As his lamp caught the match flame the dogs growled in the doorway. "Good fella! Good girl! But out now, come on, out." He eased them into the lean-to and pulled the door tight.

His glance slid around the little room – god what if – but his hesitation broke before it stopped his movement and he shrugged off his sheepskin and was at the table, tugging, prying for a hold. Finally his hand found a doubled limb; he braced himself. Gelidly a knee rose, straightened; the other leg moved as hardly, but moved, and he could thrust up under the parka to feel a bare warmth seemingly hugged together there. He edged farther, searching, his fingers felt a frazzle, prodded roughness that suddenly slipped like grease. He jerked back, knowing before the light etched his bloody fingers.

Herman saw the red smudge, blackening, the familiar room opening into darkness. He shook his head; come on, blood is blood, everybody has it – but who expects a frozen lump – the tracks, maybe there were sleighs on the road just before – it was warm! Swiftly he unbent the arms and pulled back the head. An Indian, about his own age and, perhaps, alive – breathing, yes. He stretched for a dishcloth behind the stove, plunged it into the water pail and began wiping the dark face. No cut in the shaggy parka; maybe wounded inside a house. Maybe dropped for dead.

The man twitched. Suddenly, his head jerked his cheek down against the table and his muscles knotted in spasms here and there;

stomach, thigh, shoulder, ankle. Herman held him to the final long shudder, and the limbs relaxed. He got the bottle of whisky from the cupboard then and took one long swallow. Only the features remained contorted, the mouth hanging open a little.

Night had long since thickened the storm when Herman finished bedding his stock and returned to the house. On the hides beside the stove, the Indian had not moved. Unconscious; or dead? Sleeping. Thick hair in a jagged cut at the neck; skin almost transparent over sharp bones; he knew all the Cree on the reserve across the Wapiti River but this man – he looked starved. Perhaps he was no Cree.

Tossing off coat and mitts, he washed and pulled back the blanket to study the sprawl of dried blood gluing the shirt against the chest. There it couldn't be fatal and it wasn't bleeding now, so frost-bite. The long fingers seemed all right, curled like that. He pried at the moccasins; worn out, almost, and the skin blotchy to the ankle.

He was testing a basin of lukewarm water with his finger when his glance met the Indian's, eyes wide, staring. The pupils shone as strangely, intensely black and unblinking as two polished knobs on some wooden – Herman shuddered. Then the broad nostrils flared in breathing and he said, "Hey! You're lucky I was crazy enough to try going to town. You okay?"

The eyes did not waver.

"I was crazy, yeah, and to stop too," Herman laughed, too loud in the little room and he turned to pull up a bench. "You'll have to be higher so I can try with those feet." He lined two chairs against the bench; the other shifted an arm feebly and Herman stooped, "Just easy with it, easy." He lifted him, holding his torso rigid, and eased him to the bench so that below the knee his legs hung to the floor. He got the basin and began bathing the icy feet.

When he had changed the dirty water twice the blotchiness seemed to be fading. An enormous hunger suddenly moved in him. He propped the Indian's legs so that his feet hung free in the water, then got out meat and bread. In the pan the meat spit, its aroma drifting through the smoked moosehide smell, strange in this room. He offered him a piece of meat on a fork; he gnawed as if it would stick in his throat. Herman dipped some break in milk.

When the Indian had eaten bread and, with his head supported, drunk some milk laced with whisky, Herman soaked away the shirts and the filthy scarf. A wide gash lay across the left lower ribs, glancing off one and then another. Blood welled in red beads here and there but, oddly, it seemed clean, inflamed only at the apex. He got his medicine box and fished out the needle and catgut boiling in a pot on the stove. Even for his stubby fingers the heavy gut fit the needle easily. "This is just for cattle, you know, but it works. Fixed my leg good, once, when a crazy boar ripped her from here to here." He reached for the iodine, and the Indian's look flicked up at him, abruptly alive and blazing as the blizzard roared outside. But as swiftly his eyes closed, and he said no word. "Hey," Herman said, "you better have some whisky, straight."

After, he cleaned up and sat down at the kitchen table, elbows spread wide. The bay shying and his own stupidity, as he thought it then, at getting out to see what it might be and the instant of terror, as totally violent, as totally strange to him after all the Saskatchewan blizzards he had outfaced, when the track vanished under his feet just before he saw the drift forming over the mound – he was not even sleepy, now. The storm whined about the cabin. In eight years no one but himself had ever slept in the bedroom until a half dead – aw, he had done with those thoughts. No one visited him; that fact required no thinking. No more than the deacon's remembered voice when, at Herman's persistence in marrying his daughter, he had named him the bastard of a woman long since dead and left him to stumble out, past the mute face of the church minister, into that long ago summer night. His washbasin mirror had stared back at him and his face bloody with mosquitoes crushed in the trudge home.

He stirred. The things he had brought from town: he had ordered them long ago, carefully, and risked a dash to town before the storm for them, but now they could wait. He piled packages and mail on the table, and a magazine cover made him pause. "Christmas is coming," it stated. A doll lay among blankets; through the frosted window behind it stared in a child's face. Round eyes staring at the doll white as frosting. After a time he roused: the title was high enough, trim it and hang it up. He flipped the page; just a poem centred in a grey outlined barn and he had already begun the tear when he saw the title and first line.

"The Oxen." "Christmas Eve and twelve of the clock." His glance slipped down the stanzas: he had never heard of Thomas

Hardy. It was short so he read it deliberately. At the third stanza
he was shaping the words under his breath,

>   ... Yet I feel
> If someone said on Christmas Eve,
> 'Come; see the oxen kneel
>
> 'In the lonely barton by yonder coomb
> Our childhood used to know,'
> I should go with him in the gloom,
> Hoping it might be so.

'Barton' and 'coomb' were explained at the bottom of the page.
He could not remember when he had last read a poem. And
impossible too. Maybe when he was very small, the arms of who
he then believed his mother around his chest, her warm chin on his
shoulder while what he then believed to be the flat German voice
of his father murmured on about Jesus, yes, born in a barn on such
a night, yes – maybe then. But his barn now, the two heifers, his
yearling – old Brindy buckling to either heaven or hell! – he roared
aloud before he remembered the Indian.

Almost eleven. The poem was as good as an evening verse. He
got up, stretched, listening to the dark bedroom. Strange smell
they always had, different from any white. Not just dirt; Mrs
Labret was as clean as they come but you knew it walking in the
door. A whiff of alcohol, a snore audible above the storm; strange
too, here. He stripped to his underwear, flicked the hides straight
and, rolling his sheepskin into a pillow, snubbed the lamp and lay
down.

Firelight wavered against the ceiling. Shapes of Indians stumbling, sticking out legs and arms like sticks toward barns sway-
backed under snow where cattle leaned, legs tucked under them,
before cribs piled with hay. Strain as he would, there was a weight
on his shoulder; he could not see what his tangled exhaustion
seemed to insist. And, as the blizzard continued worrying at the
house, his grimace faded to vacant sleep.

II

Next morning the Indian's gaunt body shook in fever. After
redressing the wound, Herman wallowed into the storm to feed his

77

stock. The yearling nuzzled his sleeve and while it ate mash he scratched its ears. The white markings lay on its broad curly face in perfect symmetry. To hunt deer was impossible, and he no longer raised pigs.

Abruptly he untied the rope, tugged the pail away, and led the big calf out. It plunged about in the wind's bite, butting him playfully as he dug at the toolshed door. In a surge of emotion he wrestled it a moment, its body big and flinging, then he got his arms clenched around it and tossed it bodily into a drift. When it gambolled up he had the door free. Inside he put down the pail and, snorting, it re-buried its nose in the mash. He reached for the mallet on the shelf; just as the yearling began raising its face to him, he struck down hard.

III

Two days later noon sunlight blazed through the iced window onto the table between them eating. The Indian could sit and so there was no longer need for fresh beef borscht. Herman watched him work at the heap of steak and bannock. Like a hammermill, but silent, without a pause as if there would never be ending until there was nothing. His wide mouth no longer pulled so gauntly against his teeth and he limped without apparent pain. But then he had never shown pain. And since that momentary flicker of – what it had been Herman was no longer sure; sometimes he wondered whether he had not been hoodwinked in what he thought he saw that night, threading the needle. Since the fever the man had muttered perhaps ten words to necessary questions, face expressionless, black eyes blank beyond reach. Sometimes it seemed to Herman the man was not even there; he would come in and the house as silent, as empty as ever, and he would look into the bedroom: the Indian lay on the bed, face empty, staring nowhere. Well, the beef disappearing was proof! He grinned and said,

"You from the Cree, over the river? I don't think I ever saw you."

The other held a last piece of meat speared on his fork. "No."

"What's your band then?"

The pause stretched. "Chipeweyan."

"That's a long way north," Herman wiped bannock around in his plate. "Real cold too this winter, so early too. Hunting?"

"Yeh. No deer there."

Finality in his tone, almost like resentment. Herman pushed the dishes together. When he looked up the other's glance slid away.

"No deer," the Indian's voice repeated behind him.

"Man. And a family to feed too, eh?" But the other said nothing.

He was placing the last dish in the cupboard when the dogs barked outside and he went to the door. Two figures plodded over the blinding drifts. Herman squinted; the dogs were silent now, leaping about them. In the immense cold the world shone with a hard, implacable brilliance, lifeless in a sheer light with which the sun seemed to have little or nothing to do. It hung above the bush line like a fried egg frozen upon the sky.

No one was at the table when he turned, and it was a moment before he could make out the Indian standing in the bedroom door. His parka, which had padded the chair, he clutched to his chest. Herman said, "It's two men. I can't see who but – " and then he realized that the expression on the Indian's face was terror. Its very density seemed to hunch him together so that the shirt of Herman's he wore hung even more baggily, his body coiled to leap into flight. Herman said quietly, "From the dogs, one of them – " but stopped. In two and a half days the man had slept or accepted bandaging, spoonfeeding, washing of frozen feet, lying aloof and motionless as if waiting for his body to get over its weakness and catch up to wherever his will had long since been. No emotion; not even a twitch when iodine touched the sewn wound. Now, this, as they stood, hearing the approaching sounds. The unbalanced door scraped; the Indian was gone.

Feet stomped outside and he thrust open the outer door.

"Hello, Herman."

"Hey!" his breath caught in his throat. "Hello, Bill. Hello," to the other shape against the unbearable snow. "Come – come in, outa that."

"Thanks." They kicked off their snowshoes and the room was packed with them. Herman pushed forward two chairs.

"Sit down, warm up."

Bill was fumbling with buttons, "Christ that sun's awful. Even with the glasses I'm blind." His mackinaw opened to a vee of scarlet police tunic. "Herman, this's Constable Brazier, from Saskatoon."

The constable was tall, younger than the corporal and his blistered face drooped at a long, heavy jaw. "How do you do," he said in a strangely toneless voice.

Herman nodded. "You never hiked all the way from Hany?"

Bill groaned, "I bet. We had to leave the snow rig at the road, your drifts are damn well over the trees!"

"And it's quiet on foot." Herman laughed, "Except for the dogs!"

Bill's laugh bounced about the room. "Yeah, dammit, I guess I forgot them dogs!"

"They haven't forgot you – "

"Why are you so concerned about our coming quiet, Mr. Paetkau?" The dry voice was the constable's.

Herman glanced at him momentarily, shrugged. "Dunno. Guess we, Bill and me, try to joke sometimes." He turned to the stove. "Anyways, it's cold. I'll heat some borscht."

"By god that's what this god-forsaken cold needs more people with a pot of borscht on the stove!" Bill got out of his coat entirely. "You might as well have some too."

There was a brief silence before the constable answered, "I'll check the barn in the meantime."

Bill said heavily, "Look, there's hardly – look Herman, we're – "

"Sure," Herman swung around, poker in hand, "go ahead." Brazier, already at the door, stopped as Herman followed him.

"I won't need help."

"I wasn't coming – it's just the dogs." The growl that greeted the policeman faded at his: "Let him alone, you hear. Mutt!" The dogs sat down again, ears cocked at the black figure pushing into the glare.

Bill stood before the picture tacked by the bedroom door. "Nice," he cleared his throat gruffly. "Coming all right, hmm. December 24 and a cop hasn't even time for a Christmas picture."

Herman went to the cupboard. "I'd join you but I only got two bowls."

The corporal swung around, "Look, this Brazier and his – he's okay all right. It's just his first big job, just out of Regina and head crapfull of theory. You know." They had known each other since Bill Gent's first Treaty Day in Hany more than two years before when Herman, one of the few whites who spoke any Cree, helped quiet a brawl behind the livery barn.

"Sure. Who you looking for?"

"A Chip from west of Reindeer Lake, name of Carbeau. His sister's Joe Sturgeon's wife – you know, Joe, Stony Point camp. He came there the day the blizzard started, had a fight and Joe got killed and Carbeau got away on a stolen horse. They say he's cut pretty bad."

Herman stirred the soup. "What'd they fight about?"

"That's the funny part. It started when Carbeau got there, right away, but nobody'll say why. Yet. Maybe Joe was beating up his sister. She wouldn't say but she looked pretty bad. You ever hear of Indian men fighting about that?"

"Huh-uh."

"Yeah. Well, maybe them Chips up there learned real fast from the whites," Bill guffawed. "They steal about like them anyway. More likely Joe owed this Carbeau meat from last year. Reports are there's nothing of anything around Reindeer this winter, not even rabbits."

Out of the corner of his eye Herman saw Bill's bright scarlet move from the bedroom door; perhaps he was now looking to the bracket above the table, at the alarm clock there, or the faded gothic letters on the Bible. But it was in the room like a presence, that abrupt unfathomable terror, seeping through, choking the room. Bill talked on,

"... relatives cut him off back north and they just about had him this side of Poplar Lake when the blizzard hit. We found the horse dead on the road this morning three miles west with a leg bust. He probably tried walking this way. You see any sign of the poor dev –"

A growl flared outside and Herman sprang to the door. "Mutt! Drop it!" Brazier was stooped at the door of the kennel, his gloved hand clamped rigid in the dog's jaws.

The constable straightened, face livid. "That's a vicious dog. Ought to be chained." He was rubbing his hand. "And that one followed me every step."

"I don't keep them for pets."

"Look, I'm no prowling Indian – "

Their looks met, held, and fury roiled in Herman. "You figure they should know your uniform?" Then he saw the constable's track around the house. "If you looked at tracks you'da seen there was just dogs around the doghouse. It'd be pretty cold in there, through a storm."

Bill in the doorway was looking at him oddly; he had said too much. Too much? It was impossible. Even if he wanted to.

"The borscht's hot," he said, turning.

The two policemen ate quickly, silently, and in a few moments Bill pushed back. "Thanks Herman. That old touch is still right there!"

"Yes," Brazier said. "I've never tasted it before, but it is good. Thank you."

Herman nodded. Take him and get.

Bill said into the awkward hush, buttoning his coat, "Yeah. As I was saying when the dogs caught Brazier – ah – " he snorted, "redhanded, you get home before the blizzard?"

"Huh-uh. It got me a couple miles south of the church."

"I figured. See any sign of Carbeau?"

So say it so they get. He opened his mouth and met the tall constable's look; cold, as if performing some drill of inhuman precision. He said to Bill, "I can't say nothing that would be enough for him."

The policemen glanced at each other. For a moment only the fire snapped in the stove. Bill jerked, "All right, take the bedroom, I'll get the cellar."

Staring down at the cabbage stuck to the rim of the borscht-pot, something turned over in him and he felt spent, filthy. When they came in the door he should have just said, 'The bedroom. Sic' em' to that long-jawed – Brazier had not come out. He twisted, peered into the bedroom. The constable was dropping the end of the cot, turning irresolute, eyes probing the tiny room. If he's got a nose he can smell him! After a moment he came out leaving the door ajar. His glance circled, moved to the ceiling and Herman heard him catch his breath.

"Where's your ladder?"

"Huh?"

"Your ladder, for the attic." Herman stared at him and the policeman seemed almost to smile for the first time. He said, "I want the ladder to get into your attic. Understand?"

In his absolute confusion Herman nearly laughed. "It's just a loft, a little – I don't – " the other's look was hardening. "Stand on a chair – "

The constable jerked one around, stepped up and nudged the trap-door with his hand. A shower of dust fell in his face; he started as if a current had struck him.

"That's enough." Bill stood on the cellar steps, pushing away his flashlight. "Nobody's been there." As the other two stood motionless he emerged entirely and pulled on his mitts. "You seen no sign at all eh, coming home?"

Herman lied, without comprehension, "No."

"I'm sorry, Herman," the corporal hesitated, his face mottled red. "It's my fault. The first thing you're supposed to know in this job is who to ask and who to search. One of the drivers ahead of you on the road remembered his horses shying somewhere after the church, but he hadn't thought much of it. We never found nothing; I knew you'd of stopped if your nags shied. All right! Thanks again for the borscht. So merry Christmas!"

Herman watched them slip on their snowshoes. His eyes followed them across the clearing until they were lost in the unrelenting whiteness. There was no sense anywhere, neither his lies nor the nothing in the bedroom. Or the world with its inhuman, mocking whiteness. He turned back at last into the black house and he did not know how long he stood arms propped on the table, head hanging, before he knew the Indian was again in the bedroom door.

"My god," he said, and sat down.

Carbeau limped to the other chair. "Never saw behind the door."

They looked at each other; laughter burst from Herman, a roar that fluttered the cupboard-curtains and hushed. The other smiled. Herman exclaimed suddenly, "They won't quit, what's the use running? It'd be a year or two for manslaughter, at most. Why didn't you come out?"

Carbeau's lean finger poked along the edge of sunshine on the oilcloth. "Why didn't you say?"

Herman said, finally, "I dunno."

After a time Carbeau said, "I was getting to Labret's now." He nodded slowly.

"They wòn't come back – " but stopped. "You know them?" he asked irrelevently.

"My uncle."

"Hey, I thought they're Cree. Didn't he say – "

The Indian was looking away. "Yeh. My uncle."

Herman stood up heavily. "You'd better sleep, and start when it's dark."

He put on his barn coat and went out. He cleaned the barn thoroughly for the first time since the storm and, as the sun set, did the chores. He returned to the house and heated the last of the borscht. When he went into the bedroom, Carbeau awoke and they ate supper. Herman said, as they finished, "Even five miles with them stitches – well – if it don't open, take them out in two, three days. Mrs. Labret can do it." He pointed to the worn knapsack he had gotten from the bedroom. "There's some meat and bannock. Labrets don't have much. Here, you'll need another shirt."

The other was staring at him and Herman continued, almost loud, "Hey, where's your gun? You run your deer down?"

Carbeau said slowly, "In the fight – I – "

"Sure sure," he got up and reached above the door to the gunrack. "I don't need both. Some shells," he rummaged in a drawer, "here, you can bring it back when – when you don't need it."

Carbeau stood looking down at the little mound of things. "You better start," Herman said. "You ain't going fast."

When Carbeau was dressed at last, the knapsack on his back and the gun in his hand, Herman hooked his snowshoes off the nail in the lean-to. The other man could not seem to move; then he said almost inaudibly,

"No."

"Look, it's over five miles, belly-deep! I'm not going no – " but Carbeau jerked up to him, dark face contorted,

"Joe, I – I come jus' – jus' to ki – "

"Hey, hey!" Herman was shouting the words out of his memory, "you'll have time to make yourself a pair! Leave these at Labrets! You hear me!"

The Indian's face slowly hardened. He seemed to stoop forward, as if accepting a weight, then turned and limped heavily out on the porch. He stepped into the snowshoes. The two dogs sat at attention as in the gentle moonlight he moved into his stride. At the clearing's edge Herman thought his figure hesitated, but then it was gone.

When he became aware of the cold, he went in. He sat at the table a long time before he got up and took down the picture. He glanced at it, turned it over and, with lips moving, read the poem. Gradually his broad face softened, as if a fathomless serenity blossomed like child's laughter in him. He folded the paper carefully and put it in his shirt pocket. He again pulled the hides before the stove, stretched out face downward, and fell instantly asleep.

IV

He awoke, lifting his head from his arms. In the absolute stillness the lamp burned, sputtering on its wick. He pushed himself up and looked at the clock. Then he pulled on his barn coat, blew out the lamp after lighting the lantern, and stepped into the frostrigid world. The northern lights flamed a path down the endless sky. He could not have explained what he expected to see as his hands pulled the barn door open.

Oolulik

In the storeroom is where I am that afternoon, getting ready two sled loads of supplies when the dogs began to howl outside. From their tone a team must be approaching so I climb out, up on the drifts that cover all but the roofs of Tyrel Bay post. The short February afternoon is grey over the snow and the wind rising in a falling temperature. Paliayak and several of his people are already beside the mounds of their houses, looking west.

In that direction we still hope. The fall caribou must have gone south there, for only stragglers came down the usual eastern branch of migration and Paliayak's camp, which hunts east and south, just made Tyrel Bay the week before. With three of nineteen people lost to the long January hunger. Squinting against the gloom, I finally make out the dot moving where the curve of the bay would have been except for the level drifts. The figure seems barely to move; there can be only two, at most three, dogs on the sled. I shout to John on the blue roof of the store, swept bare by the wind, "Take the light sled and four dogs." In a few moments he is gone, dogs running madly. I go down into the store to brew tea and stir the beans. Beans. Eight hundred pounds of uncooked beans neatly labelled "Emergency Rations" for a land without a natural fuel supply. And the one government plane that came in just before the darkness hasn't returned to correct what may be mix-up, may be stupidity. Even after soaking six hours, it takes a rolling three-hour boil to cook a potful.

Beside the stove two of the four children staying in my room because of their frostbite play intently with a ball of string. I watch them rolling the ball back and forth, the string running out like a track over the floor and then rolling up again. They are warm and full of food; the aroma of beans drifts through the store. The children play without a sound.

When the barking approaches, I go out. It is bitterly cold now with the wind still rising, but all the people are standing by the two houses watching the approach. In a few moments John draws up; he has picked up the driver, two dogs and little sled without bothering to unhitch anything. The dogs are barely skeletons. They lie motionless on the sled, and when the man lifts his face to us for a long moment I can see only starvation; then I recognize Keluah, Ikpuck's younger brother. We lift him from the sled and into the store. The little children look up as we come in, then run quickly to their mother who is in the group that follows.

After he has drunk three mugs of tea I ask Keluah in the language of the people, "You come from Ikpuck?" He nods. "Does his family have meat and fuel?"

His mouth moves, reluctantly, "No."

The circle of brown faces stirs but no one says a word. I ask, "Where is the camp?"

"On Dubawnt Lake, with the others."

"Turatuk. Vukarsee. Nakown. Lootevek." He speaks as if behind his closed eyelids he sees the grouped humps of snow houses on the long shore of the lake. It is at least ninety miles from Tyrel Bay, and there is no need to ask whether the others had food.

"Why did you all camp at the lake?"

Keluah lies on the blankets against the counter; it takes a long time for him to speak. "Some deer came last fall, but not much. We hunted, shooting stragglers and here and there a small herd. But there were not enough for caches, we always ate everything we killed. A little after the twilight came Ikpuck found a good herd at Dubawnt Lake. We killed them all, and we could again lick the blood from our hands and our bellies were full. But the others had found nothing for many days, and they camped at Dubawnt one by one when they had no food. We fished. But we have no meat since the middle of the darkness."

Incredibly, not one clear hint of this has reached the post. But there has been no movement this winter: the weather unbelievably bad and the foxes at low ebb. If the reconnaissance plane had only come after I sent John to Baker Lake in early January – but it did not and that thought is useless. Three weeks without food during the darkness. Forty-five people in six camps traded west last fall – and then I remember. "Keluah," I say quickly, "Where is the camp of Itooi?" The largest of the western camps, it contains ten people, the families of Itooi and his brother-in-law Ukwa.

The man lifts his gaunt face from the cup of broth John is giving him. "Itooi would not stay at the lake when the deer were gone. He said the few fish would give out too and we would all die in one place. He and Ukwa went south to the Front River, they said."

"Have the fish given out at Dubawnt?"

"Yes."

"Have some of the people died?"

Keluah is slowly drinking the soup, the muscles of his cheek working to control himself before his hunger. Finally he pulls back and lifts seven fingers. "I left so long ago, with the last dogs. But some had died." There is no need to say he was the strongest man left in the camp. Ninety miles in seven days, with a blizzard only two days before.

Paliayak is looking at Keluah, reading every hour of that fight in the frost-black face. I say to him carefully, "Can you make up two teams from your dogs? Are there three men who can travel?"

He nods his huge head. "We can."

"I wanted us to rest at least another day, but now we cannot. One could take four of my best dogs and the small sled to Baker Lake. If the weather holds, perhaps in three days. I could send a message to take to the Mounted Police, to fly out with food. Two could come with me, with loads for Dubawnt."

Paliayak says heavily, "It will blizzard soon – two-three hours."

"Will it be too bad to travel?"

"Perhaps." He shrugs.

I look at them all standing in a circle around Keluah who is almost slumped down, his mouth hanging slack as in sleep. They are the people of this land and they know better than I what is ahead on this trail, but I do not have to ask them if they will. "The blizzard will have to take care of itself; we have no time to wait for it." A fleeting smile touches the faces of the people. Then we move quickly to complete our preparations.

Though the wind continues to rise from the north and the

ground-drift whirls about our legs and over the dogs, especially in the hollows of the land, it does not snow and the sky remains clear. We have the moon and the trail at first needs no breaking. As I jog along this seems an ordinary dead-of-winter trip, where the only matters to watch for are frostbite and over-fatigue. Ordinary, if I did not have to keep sharp eye on my two companions to make sure they keep up even though my sled is too heavy for six dogs. And if, above all, I did not know that waiting for us were the people and that even an hour longer could make all the difference for some of them. That Paliayak's son Atchuk will get through to Baker Lake is as sure as anything can be; next to his father he is the best man in the band and with the light sled and fresh dogs he cannot fail. Except for the unexpected. But Itooi early taught me that the margin of safety on the barrens is so narrow that if the dangerous unexpected comes it is almost inevitably fatal; therefore it can be disregarded. Do your best and if it fails you will not likely have another chance. Atchuk: a hundred and fifty miles in about the time we make ninety. If the weather is even barely flyable the plane will be in Dubawnt within two hours from Baker Lake; arriving perhaps as quickly as we. They will fly immediately, beyond doubt; emergency sloughs bureaucracy aside, thank God. But verified emergencies are often already too late. That too is a fact of the Arctic barrens. For the whole matter depends on the plane. With no more dogs left in the camp, we cannot hope to get all the people out with our three sleds. Besides, the bigger the loads we haul in, the more dogs we need and the more food for them we need and if we are held by a blizzard even for a few days – and in this season we cannot expect to get away without one – then it is a question whether the food and fuel oil we are pulling down the trail now against the side-blast of the wind will be of any help at all to the thirty-five persons at Dubawnt, except to slightly prolong their pain. And as for Itooi's camp –

I stop thinking about it. If the people are to be saved at all it will have to be the plane; if it comes the loads we are now hauling will make a difference. What we need now is a mug-up. I whistle to the dogs.

My oil-stove is already warm under the tea-pail when Paliayak and Nukak pull up out of the darkness. We slump in the lee of my sled, faces near the meagre warmth. Presently Paliayak says, "Maybe the blizzard won't come. See, the lights." They have emerged as we went, out of the east and northern sky: a great white-frozen band tinged pink that flimmers and shifts over the endless level of the land. There are still no clouds, and now perhaps there will be none for a little. Under the lights the winter darkness softens and the land spreads blank around us to an horizonless silver. Once when we rested on the trail Itooi told me that lights were the souls of unborn children playing with their umbilical cords. Even after years between this land and sky, the lights can touch terror. I look at the other two and they smile grimly. "It is good," I say. "We will move until the weather turns."

We cannot do quite that. Eighteen hours later we are two-thirds of the way to Dubawnt and we must make a sleep-stop. The weather has held, fiercely cold but steady; for five hours I have been pulling with the dogs. Quickly we build a snow house, feed the dogs, gnaw some frozen meat washed down by tea and crawl into the robes. In ten hours we are on our way again, not rested but moving. And the weather holds, the temperature about fifty below. I pull with the dogs immediately as do the others but we are moving across the coarser grain of the land now and we make less than twenty miles in eight hours. In the last two the snow begins to sting head-on. We are almost to the lake-ice then and still perhaps ten miles from the camp, but we have to stop and risk the storm getting worse. We waste no fifteen minutes on a house but simply pull the sleds into a triangle and huddle in the robes in that shelter. Exhausted, we sleep. When I next look at my wristwatch in the darkness of the robe it is four hours later. Nearly noon. I cannot feel my left foot and I pull off mukluks and socks, massaging, until the pain comes back. Then I push half-erect. The wind shrieks but it is not yet full blizzard.

The wind shifts to the north-east after we take to the trail, which is lucky because the dogs could not have faced it for ten miles. Nor we. The lake, at least, has no eskers. There is still a trace of daylight left when we corner the last headland and see the mounds of the people's snow houses. The dogs rouse their last efforts and break into a trot at my urging. My leader even raises his head and howls, to be echoed feebly by some of the other dogs, but no answering sound comes from the camp. No figure emerges from the scattered houses even when I halloo as loudly as I can, running.

I stop at the first circle of houses and halloo again. Entrances blocked, I cannot see any tracks from one house to the next. I dig out my flashlight as Paliayak and Nukak pull up. Their faces are gaunt with exhaustion and without a sound the dogs drop in their traces. We trudge together to the nearest tunnel entrance. Paliayak pulls the block of snow aside; I bend to crawl, calling as cheerily as I can, "Someone from far has come for a visit," following the beam of my light down the long entrance.

The tunnel opens up into the house and when I get to the end I raise my head with the light. The beam flashes around the domed roof and against the worn caribou of the figure crouching almost at my face beside the entrance. My heart thuds as I struggle erect, the two behind me in the passage, "Hello! We've come from Tyrel Bay!" But the figure does not move, it is hunched forward over the stove, its hands palm-out to the heat and even as I lean forward I comprehend the house is dead cold. Paliayak's face emerges out of the entrance hole as I touch the shoulder. It topples like a stone; Turatuk, frozen rigid.

We stare at the face fallen over in the dirt against the empty oilcan, the body visible here and there through tatters of fur. No sound at all in the house, not even our breathing, and then I remember the sleeping bench along the back. Only a bumpy robe; I jerk it back and there lie Turatuk's wife and his seven-year-old son and baby daughter, in a row, as they slept.

Paliayak and Nukak have not moved out of the entrance. I fling the beam of light around the small house, but there is only the useless tin stove, dog skulls, bones, the empty oil drum, a few scattered pots, and the bodies. They have eaten everything – extra clothes, hides, the very dog bones are split for marrow. Someone has chewed the leather braided handle of Turatuk's dog whip. I say, "The other houses – there must be some still," and Nukak plunges out of sight with Paliayak behind him.

We go the round of the death encampment. In some houses weak voices answer when I call at the entrance and we crawl in. We empty one of the larger houses and Paliayak and Nukak help or carry the living to it, setting up stoves and melting snow and heating meat while I run on, from house to house. I find several where the people, though alive, cannot answer my call so each must be searched. The darkness has long come when I have finished all the houses I can find. Of thirty-five people who should be here, we have found seventeen alive. Of the men only Ikpuck and

Nakown remain; the hunters inevitably go first. I squat beside Ikpuck and in his face I cannot see the brightness of the isymatah, the leader of his people. He says, in my silence, "We sent Nayak to you in the middle of the great darkness. Then at last we sent also Keluah."

"Yes. Keluah told us. But Nayak never came."

"Ahhh," it is a sound deep in his throat.

"Ikpuck, we have searched all the houses here, three in this group and four to the west, where you were. Are there others here? And have you heard of Itooi and Ukwa?"

Beyond Ikpuck, where Paliayak is doing woman's work, the fragrance of thawing meat fills the snowhouse with warmth and strength. Ikpuck does not move as he speaks, "One has not heard from Itooi. They were going back to camp on Front River, but one has not heard of them since the darkness."

"Yes," I say in his silence. "When the plane comes we will find them. Perhaps they have found the deer. Are there others here?"

After a moment he says, "Long ago Lootevek and his oldest son went on the hunt, but they did not come back. His wife – and his other children – are in their house beyond the others, over the little creek."

"So far away? If she is alone, why – " I stop.

Ikpuck says heavily, "She was asked to come here, several times. But she would not." As I move quickly to go Ikpuck looks up, fleetingly. "It would perhaps be well if two men went to that house."

I look at him an instant, at a loss to decipher his tone. "How many children?"

"Three."

Impossible. Outside I find Nukak unloading the last from my sled, and in a moment we are beating west along the shore. Under the overcast the wind drives like needles across the lake; it must be clear tomorrow if we are to expect the plane from Baker. One or two of the seventeen may not recover, but the rest surely will. And if Itooi's band has escaped with only one or two deaths and if Lootevek's wife and two children, or perhaps even three, remain, why out of the forty-five that had traded west at Tyrel Bay last fall twenty-seven or even twenty-eight are alive to – but I cannot face the thought at the moment: nor the fact that in ninety miles of travel we saw only two rabbits, no owls or fox tracks; nor that as far as I know only two men and three teen-age boys are left to this group of the people. I think rather of the people as they were last summer, happy, friendly, laughing together with their friends in the sunshine on the bay when the land briefly burst open with flowers. I rub the frostbite on my cheek. It seems very long ago since I heard their laughter.

"There," says Nukak as the lead dog barks, then all howl in chorus. A small mound barely pokes out of a drift. We drive up, the dogs hushing. Lootevek always was a loner and his wife, a large strong woman, hardly even smiled, but in the camps he seemed to lose some of the moroseness which fell on him when he lived near the store. I brace myself and push aside the entrance block. "Hallo! We have come from Tyrel Bay," I call, bending down into the tunnel.

And suddenly out of that black tunnel rises laughter.

The sound echoing in the narrowness is beyond measure more horrible than the silence we expect. I stop and Nukak's scramble behind me ceases. I cannot unravel thought; I can only shout, "We are coming," and lunge forward, Nukak at my heels. The house is dark but I fling the light-beam up before me and we are inside. It is as cold as the other houses, but on the sleeping bench Lootevek's wife sits erect, wearing her outside parka, her eyes glaring through matted hair, her mouth still hanging slack from the sound which greeted us. We stare at her. I move the light, but she is obviously the only person in the house.

"Where are the chil – " I begin but Nukak jogs my arm, gesturing to the floor. There are so many split bones lying about that I stumbled coming in. As I blink down at them now suddenly the woman laughs again. And in that shriek I understand.

There is no way to get her from the house but tie her in the sleeping robe and kick through the wall to the sled. We bring her to main camp and put her in a house by herself where her laughter will not terrify the rest of the people. Then, after several hours of feeding broth to those who cannot sit erect, I crawl into my sleeping bag.

Paliayak rouses me after eight hours; we go out, and clearly the blizzard that has been holding off is moving in over the lake from the north and east – the direction of Baker Lake. No plane on earth can get aloft in that. There is nothing to say, so we go back in and heat food. As we eat I explain a plan. He shakes his head, but helps load the sled. He stands looking after me as I urge the rested dogs out on the lake. Perhaps, with a light sled and rested dogs, I can cover the twenty-odd miles somewhere along which Itooi's Front River camp may be before the weight of the storm hits. And if forced to stop I can wait out the blizzard as well on the trail as in this dreadful camp. So we run.

When the blue shadow that precedes dawn comes up over the long white land breaking trail for the dogs is no easier for the wind rises inevitably, nagging loose snow, and the bank of cloud more clearly rolls higher behind me. About dawn I make out the ridges on the lakeshore between which the Front River breaks to the lake and I turn south. Once on the twisting river I cannot lose my way: I simply follow until I reach the camp. If Itooi has left the river – well, it is useless to think of that.

The diffuse sun-blob is as high as it will rise when between the van lashes of the storm I think I hear the echo of a plane. I am chewing meat as I run, not daring to stop for tea, but at that I stop and tear back my hood. There it is again! I stare around, the blood pounding in my head, searching for direction from the wind-torn sound. The dogs prick up their ears, and then I see the flash of it, between tags of drift, coming up over the esker from the south-east. I jerk the covering from the sled, clamber up a rock ridge and wave frantically. The snow swirls around me and the plane noses on obliviously west and north. Then, suddenly, it banks towards me. A red and silver Norseman; they must have radioed from Baker to Churchill and they risked a try into the storm. The plane roars over and I wave north-east towards the lake. It circles right, red light flashing. Don't be so stupid! And you know there's no place to land on the river bed or on the ridges! He passes over again, very low, so slowly the stall warning must be roaring in his ears. He dips and I see his face: Jimmy Hughes of Churchill. Swinging the tarp towards the lake, I scream at him though he cannot hear me, and he lifts up again into the wind. The wings waggle. He understands; and knows as well as I he's daring the face of the storm to try and unload, take on some of the people and get out before he's grounded. In a few moments he will be over the camp from which I've been struggling four hours. If the storm had held off we could have searched – but there is no need for such thought, and I clamber down to the team.

Two hours later it is impossible. The blizzard has been upon us in full fury for over an hour and only because it is behind us could we still trek. In its blindness now I realize I could go within twenty feet of the camp never knowing. And I have to stop while I have enough strength to build a snowhouse. Suddenly the dogs whine behind me. I stop, look back at them and then ahead. There is nothing except the streaking snow. I get my mitt on my leader's collar. "Okay, com'mon."

We move ahead slowly, and then abruptly the snow darkens and a shape is floundering towards me. "Hallo!" I reach for the shoulder and head bent into the white wind. The figure jerks and straightens. I am staring into the sunken frostbitten face of Oolulik, wife of Itooi.

I hold her by the shoulders then, for when she recognizes me she seems almost to crumple. After a moment I can ask, "Are you breaking trail for the others? Are they behind you?" I brush the ice from her face and she shakes her head with a shudder. "Where are they? Can we get to them before the storm is highest?"

She says through frost-broken lips, "They are in the camp by the Lake of Little Men." Somewhere beyond – perhaps five, perhaps eight miles, where the Front River runs out of the lake, where the deer cross and where for generations the people have hunted them by setting up rows of rock mounds that at a distance look like short men to channel the deer into the river for easier spearing. Three years before Itooi took me there for the fall kill; there were full meat caches that winter. I stare at his wife now, trying for a moment not to think what her being out in this storm alone means, trying not to understand the small bump on her back under the parka. She murmurs, "They are without breath in the snow houses, Itooi also. Only the baby."

For a moment we hunch there, our backs to the storm. "Come," I say finally, "we must find a drift for a snow house."

There is little time to look, and the house we manage to build is tiny. But it is shelter, and when I get the oil stove and the food inside from the sled there is warmth. I melt snow for water and give Oolulik the soup to drink from around thawing meat. She soaks a bit of hide in it and gives it to the baby to suck, but he seems almost beyond that. I should have remembered milk but she looks at me and murmurs, "Tomorrow one will have milk for him." I crawl out to feed the dogs; the storm is so intense now that I cannot see my feet. I check the dogs' chains, pull the sleeping robe off the sled and struggle back into the house. Oolulik is holding her child to her under the parka, bending back and forth over the little stove as if rocking in sleep. I rouse her. "The storm will be long, and we must save the oil. Here." I spread my heavy robe on the sleeping bench; she looks at it. She herself sewed it for me three winters before. "I know," I say at her look, "you could carry nothing but the child. But we must stay warm." I squat by the stove.

She lays the naked boy in the robe, then pulls off her own worn, frost-hardened clothes, spreads them out on the floor and gets into the robe. I blow out the stove and in the darkness I quickly undress and lay out my clothes to freeze. Then I crawl into the robe also. It is just large enough. I can feel the ice of her emaciated body against mine but I know that together we will soon be warm, and as she hunches closer the wind's whine over the house is already dying in my ear.

For the first three days of the storm we do little but sleep. Oolulik eats what she can and cares for the child. He is her only concern and as she grows stronger she has milk for him but he does not improve. She rocks him gently, holding him to her under the parka, and in the long hours she tells, in snatches, the story of what had happened at the camp by the Lake of Little Men. If we were not alone in the cramped snow house and her strong hand-some face haggard as I have never seen it, I could almost think we were in the hunting camp as we have been so often and that any moment my friend Itooi will crawl through the door and lift his laughing face to us and shout, "Telling old stories again? No one bothers with them now, only a few women! Ha! But just now a deer happened to run under the guns. Perhaps it will be enough for sup-per!" But no deer will ever again just happen to run under Itooi's unerring rifle. He lies where he has fallen over the fish hole in the ice, Ukwa's knife-wounds in his back. For Ukwa, big simple child-like man who could not hunt very well, and did not have to as long as his brother-in-law cared for him and his family, broke men-tally under the long hunger. In his madness he may have believed Itooi was deceiving him in dividing the few fish on which the two families subsisted, so he – who knows – the fact was he went to Itooi jigging for fish, stabbed him, then went to his brother-in-law's house and before Oolulik knew what was happening had already stabbed the oldest girl as she lay beside her brother. Oolulik, strong in terror, succeeded in wrestling him down and tying him because he kept crawling back to the sleeping bench, insanely intent on the ten-year-old boy, Mala. Then, the baby on her back, she went out to get Itooi to do what had to be done with the madman. She found her husband face down in the ice hole. There was only one law left her: survival. She returned to her house, pulled a thong taut around Ukwa's neck, dressed Mala in what hides were left and, with the baby still on her back, leaving her dead and Ukwa's wife – her sister – and children she could not know in what condition, with time only for one desperate effort for her two sons, she began the trek for Dubawnt Lake under the threat of the storm. But Mala was too weak; in an hour he collapsed. She waited beside the boy until his panting stopped, then covered him with snow and turned again to the storm. Some hours later I found her.

We are safe now; we have food and shelter. But it is too late for the baby and on the third day he dies.

On the fourth day she gives me the body and I take it out. Finding my marker, I dig out the sled and lay the body under it where the dogs cannot reach. The blizzard howls without cease. There is no way to help Ukwa's family even if they are alive. The storm roars over me for a time, then I return into the house. Oolulik is sitting as I left her and I begin to melt snow to make tea. We have said nothing since the child died, and I cannot endure the silence. But how to break it? We have known each other since I came to Tyrel Bay and though we are about the same age, she is my mother as Itooi has been my father in the north. Now I can only make her tea.

She drinks a little. Eyes closed, she squats on the sleeping-bench, swaying slightly. I drink tea, listening to the storm, and presently I sense her singing beside me. It is not a Christian hymn such as the people love to sing when the missionary comes to Tyrel twice a year and which they sing together when they hold their daily morning prayers. It is the old song of the people that I heard only once or twice during my earliest days in the north, a song as I have long since not been able to beg from Oolulik. Like the singers of the people long ago, she is composing as she sings, and it is her own song:

Where have gone the deer,
The animals on which we live?
Who gave us meat and blood soup to drink,
Our dogs strength to run over the snow?

Once their strong sinews sewed our clothes,
And their bones gave the sweet-brown marrow;
Then our houses were warm with the fire of their fat
And our cheeks smeared with their juices.
Eyaya – eya.

And when they would not come,
Long ago,
The angakok would send his soul beneath the lake
Where lives the mighty spirit Pinga
And there sing a charm for her that would soothe her
And the deer would come
In great herds that covered the land
And the birds that follow them hide the autumn sun.
We would hunt them at the sacred crossings
Where the little men stand guard,
And the angakoks would sing their songs,
And the people would keep strictly to the taboos
And not offend Pinga,
And in the winter the storm would wail about the house,
The dogs roll up, their snouts under their tails,
On the ledge would lie the sleeping boy
On his back, breathing through his open mouth,
His little stomach bulging round.
Eyaya – eya.

Were it not Oolulik, the wisest woman among the western people who is singing, and were her song not so terrible in beauty, I would think her mind has given way. For though she is the daughter of a great angakok and it was whispered among the people that even as a child she had already shown some of his power, she gave her name to the missionary as a young girl and all her life she has been a fervent Christian. She told me the legends of the people only after much persuading. Itooi was the church catechist for the band, leading the services during the long months the missionary could not visit them. Like all the people, they were profoundly devotional. The two times I was with them at Baker Lake they attended church services every day six days of the week. The angakok to them had long ago been declared the power of Satanasi, the devil. And now Oolulik sings on:

When all the people came safely from the hunt
Then we knew our amulets were strong,
And the angakok who had gained his strength
In the lonely way of the barrens
Would sing of Sila, the great spirit
That holds up the world and the people
And speaks in no words
But in the storm and snow and rain
And sometimes through unknowing children at play,
Who hear a soft gentle voice,
And the angakok knows
That peril threatens.
When all is well Sila sends no messages.
He remains solitary, silent.
And there is meat in the camp, and the drum dance
Calls the people for dance and laughter and song.
The women lie in the arms of the song-cousins of
*   their husbands;*
And the angakok speaks through the fire of the seance.

She has stopped, her face tilts back toward the low roof of the house, her eyes closed. Her song in its short endlessly repeating melody has grown loud, but now it drops away:

Eyaya – eya
Where have gone the deer,
And the people of the deer?
Eyaya – eya.

When I can bear to look at her again she is motionless on the sleeping-bench, looking at me with bright dry eyes. Suddenly she says, "When the white man came to the people with guns and oil for heating, it was almost as if we no longer needed shamans or taboo for we could hunt the deer wherever we wished, from far. Then the missionary came and told us of Jesus and we listened and soon our old beliefs seemed of little use for us to live. We have lived this way most of my life, and every year the deer have been less. And our prayers to God do not bring them back. In the old days the shaman did."

Finally I can say something. "Oolulik, you do not believe that. The shaman could not bring the deer if there were none."

"There always were deer."

100

"Yes, but they have been over-hunted, here, in the north, in the south."

"Because men have guns."

"Partly, but also – "

"And they no longer keep the taboo of not killing more than can be eaten. The missionaries tell us that we must believe other things, and the white men do not even believe what the white missionary says. We have seen them in Baker Lake; many never go to church, and yet they are fat and warm and never hungry. We believed and prayed, and see – " she gestures about the tiny house. "There is nothing left to believe. The deer and the people are gone."

"The people are not all gone. There are many left in the eastern bands, and to the north, and the deer will come back in a few years. The government is beginning to make surveys and soon we will know why the deer – "

She is looking at me with a gentle smile and I cannot continue. "Abramesi," she says. "You are a good man. But you did not go with us to church. You do not believe either."

Finally I can murmur, "But you have believed for many years, long before you met me. And you still believe."

She does not look at me but stares against the wall of the house as if studying the storm that howls beyond. She says at last, "The deer are gone and the people of the deer are gone. I also wish to go away."

There is nothing to be said. Later I crawl out and feed the dogs; there is only one skimpy feeding left, but from the sound of the storm it may break tomorrow. I go in and prepare food for us. Oolulik eats little, squatting silently on the floor. She will remain that way all night, swaying back and forth, singing softly to herself. I undress, crawl into the robe, and pull it tight over my ears.

I awake to the smell of food. Oolulik is at the stove and there is no sound of wind outside. I dress quickly and crawl out. Stars sparkle in the fierce calm cold; when the sun comes up the world will blaze white. In a few moments we have eaten, loaded, and are on our way. Oolulik rides the sled with the body of the child. She leads us unerringly to the spot; we find the body of her other son and take it with us also. Travelling is fast on the wind-hard drifts. In an hour we are at the camp, and even as I clear the entrance of Ukwa's house I hear the plane coming from the north. It will spot

101

the dog-team so I concern myself no further with it for the moment but scramble into the house. Amazingly, Ukwa's wife and two of the three children are still, if barely, alive. They know nothing; only that Ukwa has not returned. I start the stove, put on frozen meat and crawl out. The plane is landing on the ice of the lake and with a jolt I see it is the R.C.M.P. craft from Baker. A little luck now would have been too much to expect.

Corporal Blake must, of course, examine all the bodies. Oolulik has brought all hers to the sled, and after he crawls into what was her house and examines Ukwa. There is no way of concealing the way he died and I translate while the policeman questions her. Nothing can be done: she has killed the man and she must be arrested. It seems we will have to take the bodies of the two men with us for medical examination, but then it leaps in me and I curse him, long, completely. When I can control myself he says only, "Yes, it would be too much for the plane." And he permits Oolulik and me to take what is left of her family out on the wind-swept hill overlooking the lake. There is, of course, no way to dig a grave. We do what the Eskimos did long ago: lay them on the ground, cover them with the few wind-cleared rocks we can pry loose, and leave them to the elements and the wild animals. In the house I had found Itooi's prayerbook and now I hand it to Oolulik to read a prayer over the four graves. But she takes it from my hand and, without opening it, thrusts it under the rocks. Then, squinting against the blazing sun on the snow, we drive down the hill. Blake has helped Ukwa's family to the plane, and when we arrive the two sisters look silently at each other, one knowing, one unknowing though without hope. We climb in; four adults, two children and five muzzled dogs make an awkward load but soon we are airborne. We circle over the hill with its patch black against the snow, and head for Tyrel Bay.

Two days later when the plane comes in from Baker again to evacuate the last of the people from Dubawnt Lake, the pilot tells me that the first night Oolulik spent in jail she had hanged herself. She too had gone away.

Bluecoats on the Sacred Hill
of the Wild Peas*

"Hey, look, up ahead, the white on that hill there, that's it!"

"What?" Only his small son responded; not even this green Montana valley could nudge them from the stupor of an all-day line of Wyoming plains.

"That's crosses, of the battlefield I think. That must be where the soldiers are buried, yeah."

His wife shifted the baby once more on her tanned legs. "They just better have a campground there, is all I say, with their thousands of graves. Sheridan was plenty, but not for you, oh no."

"Yeah," he was saying again, more slowly, "thousands – looks like a awful lot." The hillside half a mile to his right came up quickly while he kept car and camper on the road by instinct, his sixty-two m.p.h. standard on limited access highway. "Too many. There were either 265 or 266 killed, but that's way too many, sure."

"There's more on the hill behind," the little girl pointed across the jumble of blankets around her.

in further observance of the occasion, Robert Little Beaver of Oglala Sioux improvised a moon dance.

"Stay on the road!" his wife shouted.

"Oh – yeah, that's it, that's the hill, the higher one where they made the last stand. This in front – hey, that was the Little Bighorn, eh?"

---

* With a certain acknowledgement to *The Denver Post*, "The Voice of the Rocky Mountain Empire; Denver, Colorado, the Climate Capital of the World", Empire Edition, July 22, 1969, p. 17.

The tires had sung loud over a bridge. His wife said, "Slow down and you'll maybe see something else."

"That in front, there, is probably a national cemetary, or something. Like the one in the Black Hills we saw."

And so it proved when they wheeled right at the sign "Custer Battlefield National Monument 1 m" and in a moment turned right sharply again up the hill to the parking lot sweating tar faintly into the evening's heat. The two oldest children converged on the running water fountain but there was no shade; and no campground.

"The museum closes in half an hour," he said, "but there's a kind of area for camping in Crow Agency up the road just two miles, so maybe tomorrow – "

"It's four nights, and today you have to make five hundred miles. I've got to bath this baby. I'm not staying anywhere where there's no hot water." The baby was beginning to laugh in the beautiful way he had which meant that in 2.7 minutes he would be screaming, whether held or not.

after man had been on the moon at least thirty minutes, the television sets were turned off and the coronation began

"Yeah yeah," he said, getting in slowly. "That means Hardin. So fifteen minutes. Hey, kids. Comm'on!"

The car pulled the little camper slowly up the steep incline. The tapered squarish monument on the highest point of the ridge stood, they discovered, on a massed grave of the 225 men of George Armstrong Custer's personal command that had been killed with him. A black iron fence surrounded the white stones marking the spots on Custer Hill where forty-two bodies had been found. The level western sun washed like a green mist of sagebrush down into the valley flat with wheatfields and twists of the Little Bighorn outlined in cottonwoods.

*as Armstrong descended from the lunar landing
vehicle, the four hundred persons in the big ballroom fell
silent when he stepped from the last step
of the ladder to the lunar surface, they let out a
whoop*

There's the valley we came up," he explained. "The Indians were camped all the way back from there where the Little Bighorn

– the Indians called it the Greasy Grass – turns right angles across the valley. The northern Cheyenne camped first, about there by the bridge, because they always led, the fiercest plains fighters but they weren't as many as the Sioux so they joined together with them against the whites, then the Oglala Sioux whose war chief was Crazy Horse, greatest of the plains Indian generals – we saw the Oglala reserve now across the Badlands in South Dakota, by Wounded Knee – and then there were some circles of other Sioux tribes like Brulés and Minneconjous. Right in the centre there was the huge sundance lodge. Remember I told you at Bear Butte that they usually held their sundances there but the settlers coming into the Black Hills, with the Army, chased them away west

>*three television sets were placed around the ballroom*
>*at the Little America, and the sight of a man*
>*stepping onto the moon held the crowd's attention*

so they held their sundance here in '76. That's why there were so many Indians in one place, may more than G.A. Custer or his general, Terry, or anyone ever thought there could be. Maybe eight or nine thousand. And right way over there, coupla miles up the valley, their camp was so big, were the Uncpapa Sioux with their warchief Gall and the chief-medicine man Sitting Bull, the greatest of the Sioux leaders, who in the sundance had had a vision of white men on horses falling into the Indian camp. That gave all the Indians courage to fight when old G.A. showed up, because they knew their medicine was good. Maybe four thousand warriors, at least two."

"It's beautiful," his wife was dandling the baby between her hip and the iron fence.

"What!"

"Everything. The hills and the sage brush – that colour – the valley and the mountains back there."

"Maybe it was like this here June 25, 1876. When Cheyenne chiefs rode into battle they often sang, 'This is a good day to die'. This was a good place, maybe."

Their little boy suddenly raced down the hill. In a minute he was back, having circled the grating with its dead-white stones, panting.

"Is that all the cowboys," he asked, collapsing on the edge of the mass grave.

"There weren't any cowboys. It was the army, the U.S. Army 7th Cavalry, fighting on these hills all over, see the stones, where cavalry – soldiers that ride horses – is stupid to try and fight. It should have been down there, on the flat, where it can manoeuver."

"That's the colour I want for the livingroom. I've been thinking about it all day and that's what I want."

He stared at his wife.

"Sagebrush, the green. Sagebrush."

"It's terrible," the little girl said. She had been motionless, looking through the bars at the stones and across down into the valley. "It's not nice to kill people or Indians. Why did they want to kill them?"

"They did manoeuver," he said to her. "Over there, at the Uncpapa end of the valley Custer sent Major Reno with three companies, about 150 men – "

"Like in Nevada?" his wife asked. "Reno, Nevada?"

"Wh – oh – I don't know. No, that was earlier – what the – "

"You seem to know everything else, that's all." His wife hoisted the baby, laughing again ominously, and went up around the monument.

"No, I don't think it was named after him," he followed her. "He never make himself famous with that charge, down the valley. They hauled him into court later because he and most of his men survived. They thought he stopped too soon. He attacked, stopped when lots of Indians charged him, retreated back to the bluffs and that left all the Indians more or less free to attack Custer and his five companies at this end. At least so some think – nobody knows for sure. How can they, the only living thing to survive of the 7th was a horse."

"I remember that," the girl said. "Comanche!"

"Right!" he grinned at her. "You can see it from here, how it happened. The whole 7th Cavalry, twelve companies, came in way down the valley from the south and east over there. Reno was ordered to attack the village – in the dust and smoke they didn't have much idea how big it was but Custer would probably have attacked anyway; he thought Indians just had to see him to run – and Custer with his five companies rides along behind these hills to attack the other end of the village – city really, it's so big – down a creek valley there to cross the river. When Reno gets chased back across the river to the bluffs – the Indians fight so hard because they have good medicine and they're protecting their women and children

Miss Powers will be next year's queen both girls
are students at the University of Wyoming in Laramie
Miss Nimmo will be a senior next year, working
toward a degree in agricultural economics, and Miss Powers
will be a sophomore

the Indians can throw everything against Custer. Gall, leading the Uncpapas, counter-attacks Custer's charge down Medicine Tail Creek toward the ford, cuts him off from getting any more messages for help to the supply train or Reno or even Captain Benteen, who's got four companies back there in reserve. Custer is forced up this slope, fighting all the way, men falling where the stones are, see, Indians racing back and forth around him, hanging low on one side and firing over or under their horses' necks. In the meantime, Crazy Horse and his Oglalas, the fiercest of the Sioux, have come up behind this hill from the north, see, there, and attack Custer from behind over the crest right here. That's why they're all scattered down there, just below the top. In probably half an hour it's all finished."

The little boy was goggle-eyed. "Is somebody dead?"

"They're *all* dead. Companies C,E,F,I and L of the U.S. 7th Cavalry – old George Armstrong too, right there by the stone with the iron flag he was lying, and the Indians whooping it up. Get in, we'll go see where Reno and Benteen got besieged."

Bottle-warmer plugged into the cigarette lighter, they drove very slowly along the ridge, its west slope washed in the green mist of the falling sun, its east dark with small white clusters of stone where three companies had fallen. Over a cattle guard in the road, and down between grazing cows toward the river and Medicine Tail Creek running high after a month of rain.

"Why are so many bodies on the east slope, if Custer went down to this ford and got beaten up the west hill, like you say?"

"I didn't know, were you listening," he said. "That's a good question. Actually, nobody knows what happened because Indians at that time mostly told whites what they wanted to hear and so their reports later – when they were convinced they wouldn't get hung for even admitting they were in the fight – were pretty much contradictory. Some believe Custer never even got near the river, he just stayed back of this ridge all along, but then that doesn't explain E Company all the way down that ravine or – hey, look! They've cut the road right *through* Weir Point!"

> *the week-long festivities began when Miss Frontier,*
> *Marie Nimmo of Cheyenne, accepted a bouquet*
> *of roses from Milburn Stone, who plays Doc*
> *in the Gunsmoke television series Miss Nimmo's*
> *lady-in-waiting, Carol Powers, was greeted by Ken*
> *Curtis, who is Stone's television sidekick, Festus*

So they had. He stopped by the marker explaining that in the late afternoon of June 25, 1876, Captain Weir of Reno's command had fought his way forward to this spot trying to find what had happened to Custer.

"Fifty feet in the air now above this spot," he said and drove through to the siege-works. They read the plaque and looked across the little hollow where the surviving doctor had set up hospital, the concrete paths outlining defensive lines.

"Reno retreated from his attack on the village across the river below there and up this ravine. Lost lots of men at that ford. This was the best position they could reach, but even so that point is higher and Indian sharpshooters were potting them from there."

It seemed that under the setting sun there was no one alive except they on the hill. On the grey line of concrete down the valley not a car moved. The baby suddenly, irrevocably, began his roar.

"I'll just run around the entrenchment trail, just a minute. Can't you plug him up?"

"It's still heating in the car, dear," his wife said. "Isn't it like the Cheyenne war cry of Triple Moons, or something?"

> *the first official event of Frontier Days, the*
> *coronation of Miss Frontier, was delayed about half*
> *an hour so the four hundred Western-clad*
> *celebrants at Cheyenne's Little America motor*
> *hotel could watch the historic event on television*

"No," he said. "The name was Two Moon."

He went alone and looked down the ravine to the ford. It looked like it: the bank far below must be one of the steepest cavalry ever tried. When he turned, his boy was beside him, and they ran together along the line where M Company had lain, down and up to the point held by H Company. There were weathered trenches, and ravines folded down to the river.

"What's the little sticks?" the boy asked.

"That's where the soldiers shot from. See, that side is where they fought their way down to the river for water – they were up here two nights and a day – and over there in the east – see the hills and the trees – that's where they came from in the morning of the 25th, when Custer was trying to find the Indians and attack." They were returning down the hollow, trotting past A Company barricade.

"They shoulda had cowboys," the boy panted. "They'da fixed em."

"It was before there were any cows around here, long before. The Army men rode horses too."

In the car the baby was snorting as he devoured his milk. They drove slowly back, past the point where Custer was last seen alive, through Weir Point. Where the asphalt bent over a little hill before dropping to Medicine Tail Creek he stopped.

"George A. and his two hundred probably charged down this hill that Sunday. When the buffalo berries bloomed on this hill the young men came here to wait for their puberty dreams."

"The whole village, with mothers and babies?" his wife was staring across to the river flats.

"That was the way to handle Indians. Custer had cut up a Cheyenne village at Washita in '69 and that made him the most famous general in the U.S."

"My god."

"Some say that's why he hurried so much to find the Sioux, before anybody else. He pushed his troopers, they'd been marching twenty-four hours without sleep when they got here. Maybe he wanted to send back a telegram that he'd cleaned up the Indians for good and all and stampede the Democratic Convention in St. Louis that was meeting then into naming him candidate for President. He did promise his scout, Bloody Knife, all kinds of things when he became the 'Great White Father', Bloody Knife said

later, and he could have made it if he'd got the message out by
June 28. The Bozeman telegraph line was only a hard twenty-four
hour ride."

the pull of the moon was heavy even in the Old
West atmosphere of Cheyenne Frontier Days as the
seventy-three-year-old celebration got under way about
the time Neil Armstrong stepped onto the lunar
surface Sunday night

"Would he have got it?"

He released the brake and the car began to roll. "1876 was the
100th birthday of the Republic. They'd just solved the Negro problem forever with the Civil War, you think anybody would have
voted against a general who cleaned up the Indian problem forever?"

"This was that important?"

"Maybe, if the Indians had co-operated. He was a hero when
they still had jobs. And for fifty years Anheuser-Busch made sure
pictures of 'Custer's Last Fight' were in every beerparlour in the
U.S."

The stubby obelisk stood black against the evening sky as they
wound along the ridge; the museum was locked. Even the water
fountain was turned off. There was nothing left but the road to
Hardin. As they passed Crow Agency the girl suddenly said,

"See, the moon."

A curved sickle riding beyond some cloud. "The man in the
moon was made in U.S.A," he said. The baby, oddly, was sleeping.

"What a time for a ten-day trip like this," his wife said. "When
the rest of the earth is watching history happen on TV."

Frontier Days Moon Walk Delays Queen
Crowning Cheyenne Wyo

"Myth. We'll watch them walk onto Mars," he said. "They'll have
that in colour."

"Living red," his wife said. She was smelling a tiny branch of
sagebrush.

"Are they going to Mars?" the girl asked.

"I like cowboys anyways," the boy said.

"Sure they're going. If they push it they should get there in time
for the 200th anniversary."

110

"We are not," his wife said, "camping anywhere where there's no hot water. This child is absolutely filthy."

"Sure," he said. "If we have to drive all the way home to Alberta."

Along the Red Deer
and the
South Saskatchewan

[To the memory of Little Bear and F. W. Spicer]

This is long ago. Before whites dared to come into our country, when they built the Big House they call Edmonton now and then Little Big House at the edge of our country and barred the doors and put cannons on the corners and let our people through one small door one at a time when we came to trade. We were camped along the Red Deer that winter for the buffalo would go there under the trees and we followed them. One day that winter Appino-kommit was gone. We didn't think about that, since he never said where he was going, or when. He was a very young man who thought longer than he spoke, and the Old Men sometimes called him crazy head because he had already led boys his own age in a good raid and the older warriors hated him because they were jealous of the coups he brought back. But we, we loved him.

After many days my young brother told me Appino-kommit had come back and wanted to see me at the Antelope Butte. So I went there. His face was burned by the wind and his moccasins worn out; I saw war in his face and I loved him. He told me he had gone three days down the Great River from the forks where the Red Deer joins it and he had found a camp of twenty-five lodges. When he said this he swung his hand flat across his throat, the sign for our enemies the Plains Cree and I was very happy. He had watched that camp till the sun went down, but then it began to snow and he had to leave because they would see his trail in the snow. He had wanted to watch them one more day, it was foolish for such a small camp to be there alone but the snow made him come away.

"We start this tonight," he said. "I want three hundred young

113

men to meet me at the Lone Tree Crossing when the moon rises. Tell them just that, no more, and they are not to talk to me today because then the chiefs will guess something and tell us not to do it."

I did as he said, and when the moon came up over the Great Lone Tree the young men started coming out of the darkness, all quiet; no one knew that anyone but himself had been called. But when they saw all the faces around them, their faces shone with happiness for they saw there was much to do. Silently we followed Appino-kommit and he led us across the white flats and into the thick trees and willows. There, where we could not be seen, we built small fires and made our quiet prayers to The Great One, asking help, and when that was done every one told the others of each wrong he had done, both great and small, so that if he didn't come back no man could say, when his deeds were told in the Great Medicine Lodge, that any shame had been hidden in his heart to blacken the glory of his death; that he had faced the enemy with his warcry and his name the last brave sound he would make.

All day we lay under the trees and at night we ran until the line of light grew so wide in our faces that we had to return to the river valley for the day shelter of trees. On the sixth night our run was short. Appino-kommit told us we should sleep till he called us, but I don't know if anyone slept. Just at dawn he came among us and said we should put out the fires.

"Eat all you can," he said. "Who can say who will eat again."

The snow was almost to our knees and the sun shone on it like fire leaping in the cold. Appino-kommit led us through the brush of the coulee and soon we heard dogs, then horses, and children laughing, and I think I have never heard so many women sing so happily or their axes ring as loud as they did that morning, but I may have forgotten it. But that day I will never forget, and we were not listening for such happy sounds that day, we were very busy. The fire of war burned in us, our enemies were there and we looked at each other and saw war paint. We stripped off our clothes very fast, everything but breechcloths and moccasins lay on the snow, a great pile of clothes and my young brother had to stay there with them. This made him very sad, but Appino-kommit said it was glory enough for someone so young to be one of a war

114

party as famous as this one would be, so we left him there smiling. I don't know what happened to him; I never saw him again.

We were divided into two equal parties, Appino-kommit leading one and Kristo-koom-epoka the other. One party would follow the coulee to where it spread out into the river valley and the edge of the camp, the other would go higher, along the edge of the brush above and then, on a given signal, both would rush into the camp from opposite directions and meet in the centre, as nearly as possible. Women and children wouldn't be touched if they didn't fight. My friend, that was the time to see Appino-kommit; you would have known as we did that he was born to be a warrior. He told every man what to do, nothing was forgotten. "The Crees make it so easy for us," he said. "Such a small camp should have scouts out all the time." We looked at each other and then our swift feet carried us apart, but I like to remember that little bit of time, to remember us all together and how I felt the fire of the coming battle jerk my heart for happiness, remember my sad young brother sitting on the pile our clothing made and Appino-kommit, our leader, his war feathers quivering about his proud head in the sunlight so bright and cold, his eyes finding each one of us down to our very hearts as we stood around him. Proud and happy.

The last legging had fallen on the pile and my brother was hardly seated when the word came and we broke into our two parties, running silently, crouched, to the proper place. I was with Kristo-koom-epoka on the left, running with my good friends down the coulee and already I could hear the roar of victory, the brave deeds being sung again in the Medicine Lodge and I thought of two eyes shining and soft skin flushed soft red as I told what I had done, I, a warrior with coups at my belt who needed to fear nothing, certainly not to ask for a girl since everyone knows a warrior needs a wife to keep his lodge. My heart was pounding so hard with these happy thoughts my chest ran sweat under those frozen bushes, and we had hardly reached our place and squatted, peering under branches past the bottoms of the hills set there like giant grey hoofs when through the morning air rang the signal. The warcry of Siksika, The People.

As in that instant before a man's hands meet to clap again, there is silence. It all seems so peaceful, the sound of singing women and children, horses just hanging there as if not yet quite gone and everything motionless and so quiet with the sunlight dancing on the snow, smoke going straight up from lodges against the river hills and into the blue sky. Then! A roar as three hundred men leap up, teeth glistening into sunlight, screaming we run, stretched out towards our enemies with our knives and plumes and spears pointing the way A-a ha he ha, a-a ha he ha, I yo ho i yo ho, Ha koc e mat, Spum o kit, Spum o kit, I yo ho, i yo ho, our voices thunder in the joy of it as lodges split themselves before our sharp knives and the enemy staggers out, snatching at weapons and falling, snatching and falling and trying to stand zipp! Arrows hiss some of us down but who sees that, we are forcing them back, they are summer flies, their clubs and knives just flies brushed aside and crushed I yo ho the joy of knife thudding in bone and blood spray I yo ho I am here now! and we hear our brothers' voices bellowing towards us above the screams and smoke and know we will meet soon to grasp their bloody hands a-a ha he ha.

But listen! There is a far sound above the roar, the screams, there, between the lodges, the white dust of snow rising with the thunder of hooves down the valley, back back! Back! Each desperate voice cries to each, back! for the open jaws of horses swirl up towards us through the snow of their running with spears and knives and warcries of our enemies bristling above them, shout to your brother that death is running us, back. "All stay together!" Kristo-koom-epoka cries, and we gain the coulee's shelter fast, and we still feel there may be hope but we must turn to face those charging horses.

You see, my friend, this is how it was. In the bend of the Great River below that small camp we attacked, where we could not see it, was the main Cree camp. So big a thousand warriors could jump up in a moment. Appino-kommit knew that early in the morning the horses are always in a camp, and he knew that if we attacked at that time it would save us the trouble of rounding them up. So the thousand warriors in that big camp he didn't know about had to take no more than one running step before they could gallop.

We could tell by the sound of guns, the Cree had six or seven and we altogether had two, that the others led by Appino-kommit were also retreating to the coulees of the river hills and we would have to get together to stand, if possible. I have told you, my

116

friend, that we wore only breechcloths and moccasins, but that is not true; I also had a shirt which I'd traded the fall before from the traders when we got those two guns in the north at Big House. It was cotton and only reached my belt but it was a great comfort to me as you will see. Ai he ha, I see it all now, the rush for our lives to the coulee, we reach it and turn just in time to stop them with arrows and a desperate charge against those horses' swinging heads with axes. Ahhh, they are so tight now stabbing around us that horses can be killed with knives, they jam the coulee so tight in their rage to trample us into the frozen ground. They charge again, and again, wheel away and charge again, and four times we meet them on foot, leaping among the foaming horses, smashing their heads, tearing off riders and gutting horses and smashing knees, smashing them down, our knives driving between ribs and gulping blood straight from pounding hearts I yo ho I yo ho I am here now! the dead piled up in that coulee so high we can't see over them, the bright sunshine and the red circles on the snow as the Cree whirl around once more, and charge again. I can taste my own blood in my mouth here they come again, the fourth charge and I hear their roar as they hurdle the dead and we meet Ha koc e mat! and I am among the horses, my enemy's arm lunging a spear past me and I have that arm, he starts to fall down towards my face and I step slightly aside, knife straight up and it is gone in him to the hilt. The horse rears, screaming, and I twist my knife out, up, and with both hands drive one long red line down through his white and bay belly while he is still on his hind legs pawing above me and his warm curled intestines pour out in one great steaming puddle about his hoofs in the red snow. That hot smell now! Down, he is down like a spilled mountain and the club of a friend splatters his rider's brains in my face and we roar with laughter. They are gone. Gasping I pull another friend from under a floundered horse.

A voice is behind me, Kristo-koom-epoka has to tell me his name for my breath roars in my ears and he is unrecognizable, as if poured over red. "Take cover," he shouts, "they'll come on foot now, with bows! Cover." And they do that, but we are sheltered by the coulee, they have to shoot high into the air and the arrows falling down straight hurt only a few.

"Friends," the voice of Kristo-koom-epoka again, "I don't think anyone wants to stay here; this place is mostly cold and falling arrows. We should go back in threes, two strong take one wounded between them, I'll go first. That way we can get back to the others. Keep close together, come now."

Like a wounded grizzly we started. In an instant our enemy answered our warcry and rushed to meet us. That wasn't the kind of fight a warrior likes to remember, carrying his wounded friend and trying to cut his way out; no joy, no joy. I only remember that as soon as we started an arrow killed the wounded friend I was helping carry and I took his axe in my right hand and my knife in my left and pushed towards the front to Kristo-koom-epoka. We stood side by side and I helped him chop our path through Cree. How long that was I don't know, but at last they drew back with only a few arrows spitting at us. We could see then not far away our other party slowly retreating and carrying the wounded as we were. The Cree tried to keep us apart, but up there on the flats they seemed to have worn off their fierceness against our knives and the terrible cold; soon we were together with what was left of our friends. About then some late Cree arrived and put more heart in the enemy, but now we were prepared for them. Appino-kommit sent all the wounded ahead and formed a rear-guard of the strongest that were left. And on the flat plain there and the one shallow line of a beginning coulee we fought for a long time, driving them back again and again until the sun was low. It was the middle of winter, but it took the sun a long time to get there. Then Appino-kommit said to me,

"You are a great runner and your legs are still good. Run ahead of us to the place where we were camped this morning. Tell anyone you find there we must meet in the tall timber we passed through last night, down in that bend. Then you go ahead there and build big fires, the Cree have all our clothing. Run, or many more will die in this cold."

So I left them and I ran. I passed the wounded ones, giving them my message. I ran till there was only one track in the snow and a narrow line of blood for me to follow.

Soon I saw someone running in front of me, not steadily but as if drunk and as I overtook him I looked into his face. He was a boy of fifteen. A shot close in had blown his lower jaw away and his tongue was frozen on his breast with long icicles of saliva and blood. I only looked once and said nothing but ran on. I saw what rode his shoulder. Soon he would go slower, and then he would stop and lie down in the snow, and then sleep. Even now some-times in a dream I see how he looked at me as I passed him, I running without bad wounds, and I could not stop to help. I saw him and the lives of all depended on me but he did not know that or what I saw and his look told me that he would feel it even when he couldn't feel his wounds any more. The heat of battle was gone and we were retreating; we had to get to fires; we had to tie up the wounded.

As I ran my heart wanted to die because I had to think of all that faced us. Without clothing, home and safety was five long nights and days away, and we had no food. Would our wounded need us after one night of this cold? Of course the Cree would track us, and get the scalps of those who fell, and they would make sure that no one survived the cold; they would be all the happier if we froze like dogs rather than on their knives with our warcry sounding. Do you wonder my heart was stretched out?

The sun was cut in half when I reached the grove where the fires were to be built, and there I found some comfort because four sweat lodges made of raw buffalo hides stood under the trees. These could give shelter to some wounded, they would gradually warm if we built large fires outside them, and the hair could be used to stuff the mouths of wounds. If any still bled in the terrible cold. After I had started the first big fire I scraped hair from one of the robes, tied my shirt sleeves tight and pulled my belt very tight around the bottom of my shirt. Then I stuffed hair inside, and I can still feel the warmth that came over me as I worked hard, doing this. And soon people began to arrive, the hurt ones first, and among them Otat-to-ye, the brother of the girl whose shadow I often tried to follow in my dreams. Any child could see he would not reach home. Blood oozed from a hole in his chest and froze on his skin; an arrow had cut through his entrails and its head was buried in his backbone. Only his great heart had brought him this far ai-ha-he-ha, our hearts so heavy.

No one said a word as we worked to staunch running blood, to tie sticks around crushed limbs. At last Appino-kommit, with the rear guard. I looked around in the firelight to see who was there, and nearly half of all those who had run east under these trees so happily were now lying, somewhere, in the trampled snow. And of the ones here, over half were badly wounded. But as I looked around I had more courage; in every face burned fierce resolution

119

and revenge; o the early summer sun, may these Cree live long enough to see that! And before dawn our trek had to begin, the strong helping the weak, and those who had died at night we placed in a line against trees facing where the enemy would come so that they could, even in death, glare at the enemy they hated now more than ever.

I and a friend went to Otat-to-ye and lifted him to his feet and, each of us with an arm about him, held his arm over our shoulder with the other hand. We have moved this way only a few steps when he asked us to take him back and place him on the ground beside the dead fire. We did that. Then he said, "Take half of my breechcloth and cover my face." I did that; then he said, "Go fast, the Cree will soon be here, go fast and don't look back."

As we went I heard his voice again, I could barely hear it calling my name. He said as I stood by him again, "Take the cloth off." I did. "Kiss me," he said then, and I did. His eyes were wide open and so black I could look through them and through his skull and see the very inside of blackness. "Now put the cloth back, I don't want to see them." And I walked from him again, and I heard nothing behind me.

Friend, can you know how I felt? Do you know pain? That was what made us men, then, such happiness and such pain, that could turn quickly as a hand turning. Our hearts had to know and hold both, and though we were very young we were the children of this land and sky and we did not cry out and make women of ourselves by groaning and cutting ourselves. We were already cut enough; our hearts could bleed in silence. I see by your face you understand some of this; the story I would have to tell his sister, that I had left him alone to wait for their knives because I could not kill him. All day they ran our flanks like wolf shadows on the snow and happy the man whom the wolves got before they, our enemy. And as the sun sank Appino-kommit came and said I would have to run again. I would have to be the one to go ahead and tell all this to our camp, and ask that food and clothing be sent.

Now you will understand about a man bringing such a story into the great camp of our people. When sorrow strikes so swift and hard sometimes a hand flies up and kills the messenger who has dared to speak such words; friend or stranger, it doesn't matter, our love for our own is so strong. As soon as it was dark I started. It was colder and the snow had begun to drift before a north-west wind and I had to run against that all night. I rested a little when I could not twist my strength any tighter, then all next day, taking only a short sleep by a fire in the middle of the day, then on for three days and nights. In the evening of the third day I came near our great camp; I had eaten only rose-bush berries as I ran and slept no more than half a night altogether, watching for what might be following me, and I could barely walk as I came in, my face frozen and legs cut by the crusted snow. I moved towards the chief's lodge, for only there was there safety for me, but children recognized me and ran through the camp crying that one had come back along who could scarcely walk and had gone to the chief's lodge. The whole camp ran together.

I entered the lodge and seated myself under the Medicine, and I will tell you what that means, my friend, for you will not know it. The door of a lodge is always towards the rising sun and the chief's bed is always exactly opposite the door, that is, against the back side of the lodge equal distance from the door if you go either to the right or the left when you enter, and the head of the bed is always to the north so that when the chief sits during the day his face is always east towards his own fire in the centre of his lodge and the rising sun. There are reasons for this. At the head of the bed on his left is a tripod, his robe rests on one side of this and under the tripod he keeps his war bonnet, his tobacco, and the other sacred things, and over this, but outside the lodge, hangs his Medicine. Now whoever comes in and sits down on his left before the tripod also sits under the Medicine, and even if he is the enemy, if he gets to the middle of the camp where the chief's lodge is and gets inside and gains that place, he is safe as long as he remains there. Once out of that place anyone may kill him, provided he hasn't convinced them otherwise. So I got in, and got under the Medicine, sitting there in the warm, safest place of my people with my head hanging to my knees, and I couldn't say anything as the people ran together outside.

For a long time the chief sat with his head bowed. He had not said a word when I jerked open his lodge door so naked and bloody, and he said nothing while the sounds of people outside grew and one by one the councillors came in silently and looked at me and seated themselves on my left. At last the chief reached behind him for his tobacco board and prepared a pipe of tobacco and slowly filled his great pipe. He passed the pipe to one councillor, who placed the stem in his mouth, turning the bowl towards another and that one took a live coal from the fire and placed it on the tobacco. When it was lit, the councillor passed the pipe back to the chief. He pointed the smoking stem toward the rising sun and prayed to The Great God, to the sun, stars and moon, to earth and sky and water, that they have pity on his people. Then he passed the pipe to me; he bid me smoke, and called his women to prepare food. When I had smoked and eaten in silence the chief took my hand and said,

"Do any live?"

"Yes."

He repeated my answer to the people.

"Are they in danger?"

"Yes, from starvation and wounds."

"How far are they?"

"In two days they should be here, those still alive."

Again he cried this out to the people, and orders were given that warriors take food and robes to them.

And then began the hardest of all. The people began to ask about their loved ones. One would enter the lodge and call a name and I would make the sign for living; then rejoicing would echo in the warm lodge and all around it from those outside, but perhaps at the next name called I, I would have to make the sign of death, or wounded, and the sounds of mourning began and soon there was nothing but that sound surrounding me. I could not lift my head under it and I heard my mother's voice asking about her youngest son, three times she asked and I couldn't answer, I had no power left to lift my hand, there was nothing left in me hearing her voice for my father was dead and she was already bent under great sorrows. But I made that sign too. And the wails grew and still I made the dreaded sign and still I had not heard that one voice, the one I loved and so dreadful now and on and on until my heart gave way. I sprang to my feet, shouting, "Don't ask me for Otat-to-ye, don't ask! How can I say his last word beside the dead fire!" And when I had said that I heard a low cry in front of me and the world turned black. When I knew something again two days later they told me fifty young men had been brought back. The relief party reached them just in time, or not ten would have returned. Fifty out of three hundred.

122

It is late, my friend, and time to sleep. That was our life then, that was what made us men, such happiness and glory and pain that could turn quickly as a hand turning. When the Old Men still taught us and we lived with the great buffalo and the rivers on this land which had been given to our fathers before us and we had the strength to breathe and run wherever our eye moved across the land under this sky. Yes, we wailed that winter in the cold valleys of the Red Deer, and the Cree, ai he ha, the Cree that summer! You see, white traders finally dared come closer to us because we were friendly and we piled our robes up against their guns and the longest of them could kill farther than any gun I ever saw. No, he was too young, it was Ok-ki-kit-sip-pe-me-o-tas the war chief who led us. And how the Crees wailed that summer along the Great River, ahhh, how they wailed.

The Fish Caught in
the Battle River

On Wednesday, May 27, 1885, south-west of the barracks in Battleford I met these two men with a fish they had caught in the Battle River that day. They had a young poplar stuck through its gills and on their shoulders, and then the tail trailed on the ground. It must of been at least six feet. I don't know what kind of fish and I forget the names of these men, but maybe they're still alive and still remember.

That's what I remember, a long dripping fish or the dust on this girl's ankle where her moccasin was cut through to her brown skin – dust, or grease on the top of long hair – but hardly ever names didn't get written up from that time. Or numbers. There were exactly twenty-one yoke of oxen in our freight train divided into two companies with a leader for each and a driver for every three yoke. That way we were supposed to form two circles together fast when we got attacked or for night, and we practised that too with the men and teams inside. They never give us soldiers for protection on the first trip, nothing, not even a guard till fifteen miles out of Battleford and the trail goes right by these big Indian reserves and we camped like that and our leaders sent in two men to bring a guard so we could come past and get in. Then this Colonel Otter sends out a squad of twenty North West Mounted Police to bring us in, but on the second trip from Swift Current we never got that close to Battleford and we sure never had time to form circles among the young poplar of the Eagle Hills when these painted feathered-up Indians were sprouting all around us, Bang! without so much as a horse-fart to warn us before they were all over like the grass itch. That was Thursday, May 14, 1885. Ten o'clock in the morning. Late enough if you've been switching ox-ass since half past five on that Battleford trail. In a half hour we'd of been stopping for a feed but there were these maybe six seven hundred Indians and halfbreeds all looking only too happy to blaze away and then nothing was ever luckier than us not having more than a few hunting rifles or they'd of rubbed us right out. I guess at least three hundred of them had rifles and the rest axes and warclubs and stone-headed clubs they were swinging over their heads like loosening up for some nice game after a short night on hard ground. I was on the last wagon and in charge of food for that part of the train. So I had one of the rifles. One of our leaders he still had his head on straight and he got up with a white handkerchief – white as it was two hundred ox miles from Swift Current – on a stick while I covered him. I guess I could of gotten one or maybe even two if Frank – yeah, that's his name, Frank – and lots of good it would of done him too, but he says,

"Cover me, Dan,"

and I guess that's the way it's supposed to be done, but eight hundred Indians, what the hell. As it turned out, there were heads worn straight with them too. They said we had to leave the oxen and everything and they'd take us men as close to Battleford as they dared. It looked to me they'd been eating a bit pinched for a while and our heavy wagons looked real good to them. We weren't more than eighteen miles out of Battleford as it was and twenty men started us in, all on horseback and us holding onto one stirrup-strap, running beside them.

On Tuesday, April 28, 1885, we were starting from Battleford to get this second load of supplies, over four hundred miles round trip, and it wasn't actually us that was so stupid. We wanted escort through the Eagle Hills and we asked for it. Both for then and when we'd get there coming back. That Colonel Otter sent a policeman with orders to either move in fifteen minutes or get arrested and our teams given others to drive. That Otter should of stayed at home, in Ontario yelling orders on parade and knitting spare time, thinking his two hundred men lying around the Battle River flats was shaking any Indian feather in the Eagle Hills. So our guys weakened and obeyed orders, and his little skirmish at Cutknife Hill on May 2 of attacking a sleeping Indian camp of over half women and children just got him eight men killed including a teamster name of Charles Winder shot through the head. He was no Custer at Washita Creek, that's for sure. And on the 14th he damn near got our hair creased and lifted too. These were Cutknife Indians, low on powder and tight in the belly. Poundmaker Crees with Stonies thrown in, and they're madder than even the Crees, any day.

We hadn't run more than a mile or so when these other Indians galloped out of the bushes on the left and stopped us. One of the halfbreeds was translating a word here and there and said they were Poundmaker Indians too, but it came out we had to either go back to camp or these new ones that hadn't been in on the original agreement would maybe shoot us right there. And there were too many of them for our Indians to shoot it out, though one or two were waving their guns around, like what the hell, let's do it! I couldn't figure this out till after a few days. Our Indians, the ones we were running beside and who had first captured us, had given their WORD they'd take us close to Battleford alive but these other Indians, the same tribe and I guess the same chief and everything, hadn't given their WORD on anything. They hadn't been there to argue and so if they felt like it they might shoot it out with their friends so they could shoot *us*. You ever hear of such a thing? It wasn't as if we were enemies or anything, hauling supplies to a army that had already tried as hard as it could to surprise them and rub them out; our Indians had given their WORD.

One of the big troubles Indians have is they've got no general who gives out orders. Even if they are stupid. Stupid orders are anyways orders, but with Indians even a really big chief like Poundmaker or One Arrow can only say,
    "This is how I think,"
but if a lot of others don't think like him then it doesn't happen. If a war chief like Poundmaker's war chief Fine Day wants to lead he makes a long speech and then he rides off and if anybody agrees with him, they follow; if not, everybody sits around looking at the ground and after a while the war chief comes back and he may still be war chief or he may not. Any Christian could tell them that's no way to run a war.

127

We got run back to the main camp and they had a council. All of them this time, about thirty of the main ones sitting down in a circle and all the other men standing around listening to the talk. Indians have any amount of time for talk. Talk, they're never rushing anywhere. We stood there too, looking out of the corners of our eyes and over our shoulders; the smell was pretty strong too, considering the leaves were out all over the hills. I wasn't looking that much at leaves then, and no dusty ankles either. This was business and the women stayed where they belong, over the hill. You didn't need a word of Cree to understand mostly what was happening. If the speaker wanted to kill us he'd dance around the circle with his rifle crooked in his arm, talking loud and fast. If he felt otherwise he'd leave his rifle or club on the ground and walk around, talking like he wanted to quiet a ox or horse. It was a long time touch and go but finally they agreed to keep us alive if nobody tried to run away. If anyone did, then any Indian that wanted to could kill as many as he wanted of the rest of us. So how do you like that? I mean us freighters weren't any tribe of Indians; we'd just been working together two trips up and down the Swift Current-Battleford trail and most of us hadn't known each other before that and sometimes you don't care to continue the acquaintance longer than absolutely necessary, if you see what I mean. We accepted the terms, of course, but I could see some of them bloodthirsty ones were counting on maybe one or the other of us trying a white act. Poundmaker talked to us then, wearing his foxskin hat like always and said our lives were safe and said we should thank God. He also gave us a nice quiet man to interpret so we would know what was wanted. When an Indian visited us and expressed a wish to kill one of us, this man always let us know his wish. They took our bedding and also my coat and vest. I had thirty-four dollars and I did not like parting with that (Scotch) but the interpreter said maybe I should let it go when one Indian was swinging a loaded rifle near my head. I did then, and the whole camp started to move south-east. A minor chief had me drive his oxen, his wife and I sitting on the front seat and he sitting behind on the supplies with a four-foot cutter bar of a grass mower in his hand, all the knives broken out except the top five. An ox-cart isn't actually that big and it bumps a lot. My Indian was sitting right behind me, that thing bouncing pretty loose in his hand going over the bumps.

On Monday, November 16, 1885, I was driving four yoke of oxen with four loads of fifty-two bushels of wheat each on my way to Regina. When I was just west of the North West Mounted Police barracks I was stopped by a policeman who told me to turn to the right and keep outside the stakes with a red flag on them. Nobody could come inside the red stakes. Going around the stakes was all turtleback, no road at all, just ruts and buffalo trails and prairie bumps. If these oxen hadn't been really trained to go by the voice alone I would have had a big job. We got back to the main road, then two miles and we were in Regina. The first words I got were, "Riel is dead." He was being hung while I was going turtleback around them stakes.

We were travelling in these five columns and about half a mile wide winding between the poplar bluffs and just out on flatter country going south-east when the guard up front rode back waving everybody back into a ravine we'd just crossed. The rest of the riders went forward, and when they came back they said they'd shot a redcoat. It was a N.W.M.P., or a scout at least, and who knows what he was doing there alone and I did not see the shooting, but heard it. He was shot in the back of the head by a Stonie and they buried him a little by carrying ground from a badger mound close by. We camped for supper about 5:30 and my Indian's wife and her sisters, all pretty young, and mother made supper of peeled potatoes, bannock, hardtack, tea, milk and sugar, all from our wagon. We sat on our heels in the teepee around the food. I at the wife's right and she saw that I had plenty to eat. They didn't know about cans so I put a two pound can of Armour's beef in front of her on a board and took the axe and cut it in half with one cut. They all looked serious but didn't move when I picked up the axe and all burst out laughing when the can fell apart and they saw what it was. I did it twice more but signed that they should leave the rest for another day. My Indian never opened one of the cans, he always gave me the axe and stood a little away like he could never be sure what might be inside those tight little whiteman's boxes. Once one lay too close to the fire and exploded; that one I had to take away and bury. I always had to take a bite too before they would, but the women were always good to me, both young and old. On passing a creek I let my Indian know I was going to have a drink and I let the oxen go

129

themselves. When I got a drink I ran to catch the team and there was an old squaw. She just had her few things tied in a bundle on the back of a skinny dog and nothing in her hand. She took me by the wrist as I went past and I stopped and she rubbed my open hand slowly all over her head, smiling all the time at me.

The third night Saturday, May 16, 1885, was very cold with maybe an inch of ice on the slough where we camped. The water was good, not a bit alkali. We were sleeping on the ground between two wagons with a canvas thrown over them. The first night we were in a tent and they gave us some blankets too but when these were divided I got none and not being much good at pushing for a place I got left to the door of the tent. Every little while a Indian would come to look at us and one of them saw me shivering and come back with a beautiful braided rabbitskin blanket under which I went sound asleep and warm and forgot my troubles. I had that only one night and between the wagons only had two double blankets for six men so two thought they would be warmer in the wagons and climbed up. We had a guard all around and every hour or so a Indian who didn't trust us come and counted to see if we were all there. All of a sudden there was a terrible racket. A Indian was standing with one foot on either side of my head, a burning piece of wood dropping sparks in one hand and using a butcher knife in the other as a pointer while he counted. Only four men on the ground – good, good – then they could start killing. I didn't move my head off my boots (my pillow), just covered my face with my hands because of the sparks and the interpreter was yelling for everybody to lie still, he was telling them again and again that everybody was still there, and after a while the guys in the wagons dared show themselves and so we were all there and everybody went back to sleep. Of course no Indian camp is ever all asleep. There's always something moving, a dog snarls sniffing around, a child stands up to take a leak, horses snuffle. There are night birds too, little night hawks that seem to split over your head with a whirrr – enough to really scare you with ghosts if you don't know what they are. There's just a shadow over your face and at the same time whirrrr. On cold nights there aren't mosquitoes and the sky lights up clear blue like a lake with diamonds. Sometimes the northern lights come too, washing back and forth over the sky all quiet. Then the Indians are really quiet.

They say they can get you, the spirit dancers up there. I'd rather have slept with the Indians and was glad I was with them in the day. Then I'd get away from the only thing anyone ever talked about in English:

"How long do you think we'll live."

All I ever said to that was,

"Maybe five minutes, maybe till our teeth rot."

We moved every day a little, talking and talking and waiting to hear from Riel. They were fighting at Batoche.

On Sunday, April 26, 1885, we were coming into Battleford with our first load of supplies and Otter sent out the police to bring us in when we sent in our two riders. We camped about eight miles from town, putting the wagons in a ring for protection, the men and the teams inside. I was put on guard on the west side and the police gave me a heavy revolver. About eleven o'clock a scout of Poundmaker's come close and having a look at us but not doing any more and so we didn't either. Everything was quiet about one o'clock, horses quit stamping and the oxen lay down with their long breathing groan, men went to sleep, police walking around with almost no sound. I was lying under a wagon with head and shoulders outside the ring under the sky, the revolver under my hand. Then I heard,

"Are you asleep?"

"No, sir,"

I said, and that was the truth or I would not have said anything.

Poundmaker was head chief of the big camp of quite a few reserves together and he was at least six feet, with very long hair in two braids hanging in front, a long straight nose and always wearing his whole foxskin hat with a brushing hanging down his back. He's the finest looking Indian I ever saw, dressed in blanket chaps, moccasins, buffalo-hide coat tanned and covered with rows of round-headed brass tacks and sometimes carrying his heavy puka-makin. It had four knives sticking out in four directions. The runners were expected to bring good news from Riel but they come and said Middleton had overrun Batoche and Dumont was wounded and going to the States. Then the Indians and halfbreeds in camp put down their arms and after a couple of long councils decided to take the prisoners to Battleford and ask for terms. The squaws came often to look at us. They did not say much, just sat on the ground nursing their papooses that were mostly naked. The children would come and look too. Sometimes the children laughed at us but one old squaw who was poor and alone with all she had tied on the back of a spotted dog let me know she was sorry for me. We were taken to Battleford in four or five wagons and just as we were ready to start a Indian struck each of us on the shoulder with a quirt. That was on the 22nd. Middleton sent a message that they were to come in or he would come down and also defeat them utterly. On Tuesday, May 26, 1885, Poundmaker and his warriors came to Battleford and surrendered without terms. The flat between the Battle River and the fort called Fort Otter was covered with the white tents of the soldiers when the Indians come out of the sand hills to the south, a long, wide column of them with the two wagons piled up with guns and rifles, every kind ever sold by the Hudson Bay Company in two hundred years, flintlocks to sixteen bore single barrelled to fourteen shot Winchesters.

On Tuesday, May 26, 1885, a soldier pulled the tent-flap back. General Sir Frederick Middleton sat on a chair north of the Battle River facing west. At about fifteen feet sat Peter Hourie on a chair facing east. The Indians sat a little lower in a semi-circle on the ground to the south. I stood about fifteen feet north of the general, inside the soldier lines. Poundmaker got up from the centre of the Indians and stepped closer and held out his right hand. Middleton sat still leaning back in his chair, so after a little while Poundmaker pulled his blanket tight and turned around and sat down on the ground again. Middleton asked why he had taken up arms and murdered innocent settlers. Poundmaker said he had murdered nobody and had defended himself when attacked at dawn which he thought he was entitled to do. Middleton asked why he had promised to help Riel fight the Queen with two hundred men, and Poundmaker said if he had promised that he would have done it. Middleton said he hadn't helped because he was scared, like a squaw. Poundmaker sucked on his long pipe and after a while he said,

"I am sorry. I feel in my heart that I am such a person as I am."

Middleton sat there and said very loud,

"Poundmaker, you are accused of high treason. What have you to say?" Then Hourie and Poundmaker talked back and forth for some time and soon Hourie made a statement.

"There is no such a word as 'high treason' in the Cree language."

The general stared at him and the interpreter leaned forward talking back and forth with Poundmaker again. Then he announced:

"You are accused of throwing sticks at the Queen and trying to knock her hat off."

All at once a fat old wrinkled woman standing with the hundreds of Indians behind the seated chiefs started to talk and scream and wave her hands. The interpreter did not interpret. You could of heard her in the hills over the Battle River. Poundmaker said one loud sound without moving and she was quiet.

Sir Fred just nodded to Peter Hourie and asked more questions.

Where Is the Voice
Coming From?

The problem is to make the story.

One difficulty of this making may have been excellently stated by Teilhard de Chardin: "We are continually inclined to isolate ourselves from the things and events which surround us ... as though we were spectators, not elements, in what goes on." Arnold Toynbee does venture, "For all that we know, Reality is the undifferentiated unity of the mystical experience," but that need not here be considered. This story ended long ago; it is one of finite acts, of orders, of elemental feelings and reactions, of obvious legal restrictions and requirements.

Presumably all the parts of the story are themselves available. A difficulty is that they are, as always, available only in bits and pieces. Though the acts themselves seem quite clear, some written reports of the acts contradict each other. As if these acts were, at one time, too well known; as if the original nodule of each particular fact had from somewhere received non-factual accretions; or even more, as if, since the basic facts were so clear perhaps there were a larger number of facts than any one reporter, or several, or even any reporter had ever attempted to record. About facts that are still simply told by this mouth to that ear, of course, even less can be expected.

An affair seventy-five years old should acquire some of the shiny transparency of an old man's skin. It should.

Sometimes it would seem that it would be enough – perhaps more than enough – to hear the names only. The grandfather One Arrow; the mother Spotted Calf; the father Sounding Sky; the wife (wives rather, but only one of them seems to have a name, though their fathers are Napaise, Kapahoo, Old Dust, The Rump) – the one wife named, of all things, Pale Face; the cousin Going-Up-To-Sky; the brother-in-law (again, of all things) Dublin. The names of the police sound very much alike; they all begin with Constable or Corporal or Sergeant, but here and there an Inspector, then a Superintendent and eventually all the resonance of an Assistant Commissioner echoes down. More. Herself: Victoria, by the Grace of God etc., etc., QUEEN, defender of the Faith, etc., etc.; and witness "Our Right Trusty and Right Well-beloved Cousin and Councillor the Right Honorable Sir John Campbell Hamilton-Gordon, Earl of Aberdeen; Viscount Formartine, Baron Haddo, Methlic, Tarves and Kellie, in the Peerage of Scotland; Viscount Gordon of Aberdeen, County of Aberdeen, in the Peerage of the United Kingdom; Baronet of Nova Scotia, Knight Grand Cross of Our Most Distinguished Order of Saint Michael and Saint George, etc., Governor General of Canada". And of course himself: in the award proclamation named "Jean-Baptiste" but otherwise known only as Almighty Voice.

But hearing cannot be enough; not even hearing all the thunder of A Proclamation: "Now Hear Ye that a reward of FIVE HUNDRED DOLLARS will be paid to any person or persons who will give such information as will lead . . . (etc., etc.) this Twentieth day of April, in the year of Our Lord one thousand eight hundred and ninety-six, and the Fifty-nineth year of Our Reign . . . " etc. and etc.

Such hearing cannot be enough. The first item to be seen is the piece of white bone. It is almost triangular, slightly convex – concave actually as it is positioned at this moment with its corners slightly raised – graduating from perhaps a strong eighth to a weak quarter of an inch in thickness, its scattered pore structure varying between larger and smaller on its perhaps polished, certainly shiny surface. Precision is difficult since the glass showcase is at least thirteen inches deep and therefore an eye cannot be brought as close as the minute inspection of such a small, though certainly quite adequate, sample of skull would normally require. Also, because of the position it cannot be determined whether the several hairs, well over a foot long, are still in some manner attached or not.

The seven-pounder cannon can be seen standing almost shyly between the showcase and the interior wall. Officially it is known as a gun, not a cannon, and clearly its bore is not large enough to admit a large man's fist. Even if it can be believed that this gun was used in the 1885 Rebellion and that on the evening of Saturday, May 29, 1897 (while the nine-pounder, now unidentified, was in the process of arriving with the police on the special train from Regina), seven shells (all that were available in Prince Albert at that time) from it were sent shrieking into the poplar bluffs as night fell, clearly such shelling could not and would not disembowel the whole earth. Its carriage is now nicely lacquered, the perhaps oak spokes of its petite wheels (little higher than a knee) have been recently scrapped, puttied and varnished; the brilliant burnish of its brass breeching testifies with what meticulous care charmen and women have used nationally-advertised cleaners and restorers.

Though it can also be seen, even a careless glance reveals that the same concern has not been expended on the one (of two) .44 calibre 1866 model Winchesters apparently found at the last in the pit with Almighty Voice. It also is preserved in a glass case; the number 1536735 is still, though barely, distinguishable on the brass cartridge section just below the brass saddle ring. However, perhaps because the case was imperfectly sealed at one time (though sealed enough not to warrant disturbance now), or because of simple neglect, the rifle is obviously spotted here and there with blotches of rust and the brass itself reveals discolorations almost like mildew. The rifle bore, the three long strands of hair themselves, actually bristle with clots of dust. It may be that this museum cannot afford to be as concerned as the other; conversely, the disfiguration may be something inherent in the items themselves.

The small building which was the police guardroom at Duck Lake, Saskatchewan Territory, in 1895 may also be seen. It had subsequently been moved from its original place and used to house small animals, chickens perhaps, or pigs – such as a woman might be expected to have under her responsibility. It is, of course, now perfectly empty, and clean so that the public may enter with no more discomfort than a bend under the doorway and a heavy encounter with disinfectant. The door- jamb has obviously been replaced; the bar network at one window is, however, said to be original; smooth still, very smooth. The logs inside have been smeared again and again with whitewash, perhaps paint, to an insistent point of identity-defying characterlessness. Within the small rectangular box of these logs not a sound can be heard from the streets of the, probably dead, town.

Hey Injun you'll get hung for stealing that steer
Hey Injun for killing that government cow you'll get three weeks on the woodpile Hey Injun

The place named Kinistino seems to have disappeared from the map but the Minnechinass Hills have not. Whether they have ever been on a map is doubtful but they will, of course, not disappear from the landscape as long as the grass grows and the rivers run. Contrary to general report and belief, the Canadian prairies are rarely, if ever, flat and the Minnechinass (spelled five different ways and translated sometimes as "The Outside Hill", sometimes as "Beautiful Bare Hills") are dissimilar from any other of the numberless hills that everywhere block out the prairie horizon. They are bare; poplars lie tattered along their tops, almost black against the straw-pale grass and sharp green against the grey soil of the plowing laid in half-mile rectangular blocks upon their western slopes. Poles holding various wires stick out of the fields, back down the bend of the valley; what was once a farmhouse is weathering into the cultivated earth. The poplar bluff where Almighty Voice made his stand has, of course, disappeared.

The policemen he shot and killed (not the ones he wounded, of course) are easily located. Six miles east, thirty-nine miles north in Prince Alberta, the English Cemetary. Sergeant Colin Campbell Colebrook, North West Mounted Police Registration Number 605, lies presumably under a gravestone there. His name is seventeenth in a very long "list of non-commissioned officers and men who have died in the service since the inception of the force." The date is October 29, 1895, and the cause of death is anonymous: "Shot by escaping Indian prisoner near Prince Albert." At the foot of this grave are two others: Constable John R. Kerr, No. 3040, and Corporal C.H.S. Hockin, No. 3106. Their cause of death on May 28, 1897 is even more anonymous, but the place is relatively precise: "Shot by Indians at Min-etch-inass Hills, Prince Albert District."

The gravestone, if he has one, of the fourth man Almighty Voice killed is more difficult to locate. Mr. Ernest Grundy, postmaster at Duck Lake in 1897, apparently shut his window the afternoon of Friday, May 28, armed himself, rode east twenty miles, participated in the second charge into the bluff at about 6:30 p.m., and on the third sweep of that charge was shot dead at the edge of the pit. It would seem that he thereby contributed substantially not only to the Indians' bullet supply, but his clothing warmed them as well.

The burial place of Dublin and Going-Up-To-Sky is unknown, as is the grave of Almighty Voice. It is said that a Métis named Henry Smith lifted the latter's body from the pit in the bluff and gave it to Spotted Calf. The place of burial is not, of course, of ultimate significance. A gravestone is always less evidence than a triangular piece of skull, provided it is large enough.

Whatever further evidence there is to be gathered may rest on pictures. There are, presumably, almost numberless pictures of the policemen in the case, but the only one with direct bearing is one of Sergeant Colebrook who apparently insisted on advancing to complete an arrest after being warned three times that if he took another step he would be shot. The picture must have been taken before the joined the force; it reveals him a large-eared young man, hair brush-cut and ascot tie, his eyelids slightly drooping, almost hooded under thick brows. Unfortunately a picture of Constable R. C. Dickson, into whose charge Almighty Voice was apparently committed in that guardroom and who after Colebrook's death was convicted of negligence, sentenced to two months hard labour and discharged, does not seem to be available.

There are no pictures to be found of either Dublin (killed early by rifle fire) or Going-Up-To-Sky (killed in the pit), the two teenage boys who gave their ultimate fealty to Almighty Voice. There is, however, one said to be of Almighty Voice, Junior. He may have been born to Pale Face during the year, two hundred and twenty-one days that his father was a fugitive. In the picture he is kneeling before what could be a tent, he wears stripped denim overalls and displays twin babies whose sex cannot be determined from the double-laced dark bonnets they wear. In the supposed picture of Spotted Calf and Sounding Sky, Sounding Sky stands slightly before his wife; he wears a white shirt and a stripped blanket folded over his left shoulder in such a manner that the arm in which he cradles a long rifle cannot be seen. His head is thrown back; the rim of his hat appears as a black half-moon above eyes that are pressed shut in, as it were, profound concentration; above a mouth clenched thin in a downward curve. Spotted Calf wears a long dress, a sweater which could also be a man's dress coat, and a large fringed and embroidered shawl which would appear dis- tinctly Dukhobour in origin if the scroll patterns on it were more irregular. Her head is small and turned slightly towards her hus- band so as to reveal her right ear. There is what can only be called a quizzical expression on her crumpled face; it may be she does not understand what is happening and that she would have asked a question, perhaps of her husband, perhaps of the photographers, perhaps even of anyone, anywhere in the world if such questioning were possible for an Indian lady.

There is one final picture. That is one of Almighty Voice him- self. At least it is purported to be of Almighty Voice himself. In the Royal Canadian Mounted Police Museum on the Barracks Grounds just off Dewdney Avenue in Regina, Saskatchewan, it lies in the same showcase, as a matter of fact immediately beside, that triangular piece of skull. Both are unequivocally labelled, and it must be assumed that a police force with a world-wide reputa- tion would not label *such* evidence incorrectly. But here emerges an ultimate problem in making the story.

There are two official descriptions of Almighty Voice. The first reads: "Height about five feet, ten inches, slight build, rather good looking, a sharp hooked nose with a remarkably flat point. Has a bullet scar on the left side of his face about 1½ inches long running from near corner of mouth towards ear. The scar cannot be noticed when his face is painted but otherwise is plain. Skin fair for an Indian." The second description is on the Award Proclamation: "About twenty-two years old, five feet ten inches in height, weight about eleven stone, slightly erect, neat small feet and hands; com- plexion inclined to be fair, we wavey dark hair to shoulders, large dark eyes, broad forehead, sharp features and parrot nose with flat tip, scar on left cheek running from mouth towards ear, feminine appearance."

So run the descriptions that were, presumably, to identify a well-known fugitive in so precise a manner that an informant could collect five hundred dollars – a considerable sum when a police constable earned between one and two dollars a day. The nexus of the problems appears when these supposed official descriptions are compared to the supposed official picture. The man in the picture is standing on a small rug. The fingers of his left hand touch a curved Victorian settee, behind him a photographer's backdrop of scrolled patterns merges to vaguely paradisiacal trees and perhaps a sky. Th moccasins he wears make it impossible to deduce whether his feet are "neat small". He may be five feet, ten inches tall, may weigh eleven stone, he certainly is "rather good looking" and, though it is a frontal view, it may that the point of his long and flaring nose could be "remarkably flat". The photograph is slightly over-illuminated and so the unpainted complexion could be "inclined to be fair"; however, nothing can be seen of a scar, the hair is not wavy and shoulder-length but hangs almost to the waist in two thick straight braids worked through with beads, fur, ribbons and cords. The right hand that holds the corner of the blanket-like coat in position is large and, even in the high illumination, heavily veined. The neck is concealed under coiled beads and the forehead seems more low than "broad".

Perhaps, somehow, these picture details could be reconciled with the official description if the face as a whole were not so devastating.

On a cloth-backed sheet two feet by two and one-half feet in size, under the Great Seal of the Lion and the Unicorn, dignified by the names of the Deputy of the Minister of Justice, the Secretary of State, the Queen herself and all the heaped detail of her "Right Trusty and Right Well Beloved Cousin", this description concludes: "feminine appearance". But the pictures: any face of history, any believed face that the world acknowledges as *man* – Socrates, Jesus, Attila, Genghis Khan, Mahatma Gandhi, Joseph Stalin – no believed face is more *man* than this face. The mouth, the nose, the clenched brows, the eyes – the eyes are large, yes, and dark, but even in this watered-down reproduction of unending reproductions of that original, a steady look into those eyes cannot be endured. It is a face like an axe.

It is now evident that the de Chardin statement quoted at the beginning has relevance only as it proves itself inadequate to explain what has happened. At the same time, the inadequacy of Aristotle's much more famous statement becomes evident: "The true difference [between the historian and the poet] is that one relates what *has* happened, the other what *may* happen." These statements cannot explain the storyteller's activity since, despite the most rigid application of impersonal investigation, the elements of the story have now run me aground. If ever I could, I can no longer pretend to objective, omnipotent disinterestedness. I am no longer *spectator* of what *has* happened or what *may* happen: I am become *element* in what is happening at this very moment.

For it is, of course, I myself who cannot endure the shadows on that paper which are those eyes. It is I who stand beside this broken veranda post where two corner shingles have been torn away, where barbed wire tangles the dead weeds on the edge of this field. The bluff that sheltered Almighty Voice and his two friends has not disappeared from the slope of the Minnechinass, no more than the sound of Constable Dickson's voice in that guardhouse is silent. The sound of his speaking is there even if it has never been recorded in an official report:

hey injun you'll get
hung
for stealing that steer
hey injun for killing that government
cow you'll get three
weeks on the woodpile hey injun

The unknown contradictory words about an unprovable act that move a boy to defiance, an implacable Cree warrior long after the three-hundred-and-fifty-year war is ended, a war already lost the day the Cree watch Cartier hoist his gun ashore at Hochelaga and they begin the long retreat west; these words of incomprehension, of threatened incomprehensible law are there to be heard just as the unmoving tableau of the three-day siege is there to be seen on the slopes of the Minnechinass. Sounding Sky is somewhere not there, under arrest, but Spotted Calf stands on a shoulder of the Hills a little to the left, her arms upraised to the setting sun. Her mouth is open. A horse rears, riderless, above the scrub willow at the edge of the bluff, smoke puffs, screams tangle in rifle barrage, there are wounds, somewhere. The bluff is so green this spring, it will not burn and the ragged line of seven police and two civilians is staggering through, faces twisted in rage, terror, and rifles sputter. Nothing moves. There is no sound of frogs in the night; twenty-seven policeman and five civilians stand in cordon at thirty-yard intervals and a body also lies in the shelter of a gully. Only a voice rises from the bluff:

We have fought well
You have died like braves
I have worked hard and am hungry
Give me food

but nothing moves. The bluff lies, a bright green island on the grassy slope surrounded by men hunched forward rigid over their long rifles, men clumped out of rifle-range, thirty-five men dressed as for fall hunting on a sharp spring day, a small gun positioned on a ridge above. A crow is falling out of the sky into the bluff, its feathers sprayed as by an explosion. The first gun and the second gun are in position, the beginning and end of the bristling surround of thirty-five Prince Albert Volunteers, thirteen civilians and fifty-six policemen in position relative to the bluff and relative to the unnumbered whites astride their horses, standing up in their carts, staring and pointing across the valley, in position relative to the bluff and the unnumbered Indians squatting silent along the higher ridges of the Hills, motionless mounds, faceless against the Sunday morning sunlight edging between and over them down along the tree tips, down into the shadows of the bluff. Nothing moves. Beside the second gun the red-coated officer has flung a handful of grass into the motionless air, almost to the rim of the red sun.

And there is a voice. It is an incredible voice that rises from among the young poplars ripped of their spring bark, from among the dead somewhere lying there, out of the arm-deep pit shorter than a man; a voice rises over the exploding smoke and thunder of guns that reel back in their positions, worked over, serviced by the grimed motionless men in bright coats and glinting buttons, a voice so high and clear, so unbelievably high and strong in its unending wordless cry.

The voice of "Gitchie-Manitou Wayo" – interpreted as "voice of the Great Spirit" – that is, The Almighty Voice. His death chant no less incredible in its beauty than in its incomprehensible happiness.

I say "wordless cry" because that is the way it sounds to me. I could be more accurate if I had a reliable interpreter who would make a reliable interpretation. For I do not, of course, understand the Cree myself.

143

The Naming of Albert Johnson

1. *The Eagle River, Yukon:*   Wednesday, February 17, 1932
                               Tuesday, February 16

There is arctic silence at last, after the long snarl of rifles. As if all
the stubby trees within earshot had finished splitting in the cold.
Then the sound of the airplane almost around the river's bend
begins to return, turning as tight a spiral as it may up over bank
and trees and back down, over the man crumpled on the bedroll,
over the frantic staked dogteams, spluttering, down, glancing down
off the wind-ridged river. Tail leaping, almost cartwheeling over its
desperate roar for skis, immense sound rocketing from that bouncing black dot on the level glare but stopped finally, its prop whirl
staggering out motionless just behind the man moving inevitably
forward on snowshoes, not looking back, step by step up the river
with his rifle ready. Hesitates, lifts one foot, then the other, stops,
and moves forward again to the splotch in the vast whiteness
before him.

The pack is too huge, and apparently worried by rats with very
long, fine teeth. Behind it a twisted body. Unbelievably small. One
outflung hand still clutching a rifle, but no motion, nothing, the
airplane dead and only the distant sounds of dogs somewhere, of
men moving at the banks of the river. The police rifle points down,
steadily extending the police arm until it can lever the body,
already stiffening, up. A red crater for hip. As if one small part of
that incredible toughness had rebelled at last, exploded red out of
itself, splattering itself with itself when everything but itself was at
last unreachable. But the face is turning up. Rime, and clots of
snow ground into whiskers, the fur hat hurled somewhere by bullets perhaps and the whipped cowlick already a mat frozen above
half-open eyes showing only white, nostrils flared, the concrete

145

face wiped clean of everything but snarl. Freezing snarl and teeth. As if the long clenched jaws had tightened down beyond some ultimate cog and openly locked their teeth into their own torn lips in one final wordlessly silent scream.

The pilot blunders up, gasping. "By god, we got the son, of a bitch!" stumbles across the back of the snowshoes and recovers beside the policeman. Gagging a little, "My g – " All that sudden colour propped up by the rifle barrel on the otherwise white snow. And the terrible face.

The one necessary bullet, in the spine where its small entry cannot be seen at this moment, and was never felt as six others were, knocked the man face down in the snow. Though that would never loosen his grip on his rifle. The man had been working himself over on his side, not concerned as it seemed for the bullets singing to him from the level drifts in front of him or the trees on either bank. With his left hand he was reaching into his coat pocket to reload his Savage .30-.30, almost warm on the inside of his other bare hand, and he knew as every good hunter must that he had exactly thirty-nine bullets left besides the one hidden under the rifle's butt plate. If they moved in any closer he also had the Winchester .22 with sixty-four bullets, and closer still there will be the sawed-off shotgun, though he had only a few shells left, he could not now be certain exactly how many. He had stuffed snow tight into the hole where one or perhaps even two shells had exploded in his opposite hip pocket. A man could lose his blood in a minute from a hole that size but the snow was still white and icy the instant he had to glance at it, packing it in. If they had got him there before forcing him down behind his pack in the middle of the river, he could not have moved enough to pull out of the pack straps, leave alone get behind it for protection. Bullets twitch it, whine about his tea tin like his axe handle snapping once at his legs as he ran from the eastern river bank too steep to clamber up, a very bad mistake to have to discover after spending several minutes and a hundred yards of strength running his snowshoes towards it. Not a single rock, steep and bare like polished planks. But he had gained a little on them, he saw that as he curved without stopping towards the centre of the river and the line of trees beyond it. That bank is easily climbed, he knows because he climbed it that morning, but all the dogs and men so suddenly around the hairpin turn surprised him toward the nearest bank, and he sees the teams spreading to outflank him, three towards the low west bank. And two of them bending over the one army radio-man he got.

Instantly the man knew it was the river that had betrayed him. He had outlegged their dogs and lost the plane time and again on glare-ice and in fog and brush and between the endless trails of caribou herds, but the sluggish loops of this river doubling back on itself have betrayed him. It is his own best move, forward and then back, circle forward and further back, backwards, so the ones following his separate tracks will suddenly confront each other in cursing bewilderment. But this river, it cannot be named the Porcupine, has out-doubled him. For the dogs leaping towards him around the bend, the roaring radioman heaving at his sled, scrabbling for his rifle, this is clearly what he saw when he climbed the tree on the far bank, one of the teams he saw then across a wide tongue of land already ahead of him, as it seemed, and he started back to get further behind them before he followed and picked them off singly in whatever tracks of his they thought they were following. These dogs and this driver rounding to face him as he walks so carefully backwards in his snowshoes on the curve of his own tracks.

Whatever this river is spiralling back into the Yukon hills, his rifle will not betray him. Words are bellowing out of the racket of teams hurtling around the bend. His rifle speaks easily, wordlessly to the army radioman kneeling, sharpshooter position, left elbow propped on left knee. The sights glided together certain and deadly, and long before the sound had returned that one kneeling was already flung back clean as frozen wood bursting at his axe.

He has not eaten, he believes it must be two days, and the rabbit tracks are so old they give no hope for his snares. The squirrel burrow may be better. He is scrapping curls from tiny spruce twigs, watching them tighten against the lard pail, watching the flames as it seems there licking the tin blacker with their gold tongues. The fire lives with him, and he will soon examine the tinfoil of matches in his pocket, and the tinfoil bundle in his pack and also the other two paper-wrapped packages. That must be done daily, if possible. The pack, unopened, with the .22 laced to its side is between his left shoulder and the snow hollow; the moose hides spread under and behind him; the snowshoes stuck erect into the snow on the right, the long axe lying there and the rifle also, in its cloth cover but on the moosehide pouch. He has already worked carefully on his feet, kneading as much of the frost out of one and then the other as he can before the fire though two toes on the left are black and the heel of the right is rubbed raw. Bad lacing when he walked backwards, and too numb for him to notice. The one toe can only be kept another day, perhaps, but he has only a gun-oily rag for his heel. Gunoil? Spruce gum? Wait. His feet are wrapped and ready to move instantly and he sits watching warmth curl around the pail. Leans his face down into it. Then he puts the knife away in his clothes and pulls out a tiny paper. His hard fingers unfold it carefully, he studies the crystals a moment, and then as the flames tighten the blackened spirals of spruce he pours that into the steaming pail. He studies the paper, the brownness of it; the suggestion of a word beginning, or perhaps ending, that shines through its substance. He lowers it steadily then until it darkens, smiling as a spot of deep brown breaks through the possible name and curls back a black empty circle towards his fingers. He lets it go, feeling warmth like a massage in its final flare and dying. There is nothing left but a smaller fold of pepper and a bag of salt so when he drinks it is very slowly, letting each mouthful move for every part of his tongue to hold a moment this last faint sweetness.

He sits in the small yellow globe created by fire. Drinking. The wind breathes through the small spruce, his body rests motionlessly; knowing that dug into the snow with drifts and spruce tips above him they could see his smokeless fire only if they flew directly over him. And the plane cannot fly at night. They are somewhat very close now, and their plane less than a few minutes behind. It has flown straight in an hour, again and again, all he had overlaid with tangled tracks in five weeks, but the silent land is what it is. He is now resting motionlessly. And waiting.

And the whisky-jacks are suddenly there. He had not known them before to come after dark, but grey and white tipped with black they fluffed themselves at the grey edge of his light, watching, and then one hopped two hops. Sideways. The first living thing he had seen since the caribou. But he reaches for the bits of babiche he had cut and rubbed in salt, laid ready on the cloth of the riflebutt. He throws, the draggle-tail is gone but the other watches, head cocked, then jumps so easily the long space his stiff throw had managed, and the bit is gone. He does not move his body, tosses another bit, and another, closer, closer, and then draggle-tail is there scrabbling for the bit, and he twitches the white string lying beside the bits of babiche left by the rifle, sees the bigger piece tug from the snow and draggle-tail leap to it. Gulp. He tugs, feels the slight weight as the thread lifts from the snow in the firelight, and now the other is gone while draggle-tail comes towards him inevitably, string pulling the beak soundlessly agape, wings desperate in snow, dragged between rifle and fire into the waiting claw of his hand. He felt the bird's blood beat against his palm, the legs and tail and wings thud an instant, shuddering and then limp between his relentless fingers.

Wings. Noiselessly he felt the beautiful muscles shift, slip over bones delicate as twigs. He could lope circles around any dogs they set on his trail but that beast labelled in letters combing the clouds, staring everywhere until its roar suddenly blundered up out of a canyon or over a ridge, laying its relentless shadow like words on the world: he would have dragged every tree in the Yukon together to build a fire and boil that. Steel pipes and canvas and wires and name, that stinking noise. In the silence under the spruce he skims the tiny fat bubbles from the darkening soup; watches them coagulate yellow on the shavings. Better than gunoil, or gum. He began to unwrap his feet again but listening, always listening. The delicate furrow of the bird pointed toward him in the snow.

2. *The Richardson Mountains,*N.W.T.: Tuesday, February 9, 1932
Saturday, January 30

Though it means moving two and three miles to their one, the best trail to confuse them in the foothill ravines was a spiral zig-zag. West of the mountains he has not seen them; he has outrun them so far in crossing the Richardson Mountains during the blizzard that when he reaches a river he thought it must be the Porcupine because he seems at last to be inside something that is completely alone. But the creeks draining east lay in seemingly parallel but eventually converging canyons with tundra plateaus glazed under wind between them, and when he paused on one leg of his zag he sometimes saw them, across one plateau or in a canyon, labouring with their dogs and sleds as it seems ahead of him. In the white scream of the mountain pass where no human being has ever ventured in winter he does not dare pause to sleep for two days and

149

the long night between them, one toe and perhaps another frozen beyond saving and parts of his face dead, but in the east he had seen the trackers up close, once been above them and watched them coming along his trails towards each other unawares out of two converging canyons with their sleds and drivers trailing, and suddenly round the cliff to face each other in cursing amazement. He was far enough not to hear their words as they heated water for tea, wasting daylight minutes, beating their hands to keep warm.

The police drive the dog teams now, and the Indians sometimes; the ones who can track him on the glazed snow, through zags and bends, always wary of ambush, are the two army radiomen. One of the sleds is loaded with batteries when it should be food, but they sniff silently along his tracks, loping giant circles ahead of the heaving dogs and swinging arms like semaphores when they find a trail leading as it seems directly back towards the sleds they have just left. He would not have thought them so relentless at unravelling his trails, these two who every morning tried to raise the police on their frozen radio, and when he was convinced they would follow him as certainly as Millen and the plane roared up, dropping supplies, it was time to accept the rising blizzard over the mountains and find at last, for certain, the Porcupine River.

It is certainly Millen who brought the plane north just before the blizzard, and it was Millen who saw his smoke and heard him coughing, whistling in that canyon camp hidden in trees under a cliff so steep he has to chop handholds in the frozen rock to get out of there. Without dynamite again, or bombs, they could not dig him out; even in his unending alert his heart jerks at the sound of what was a foot slipping against a frozen tree up the ridge facing him. His rifle is out of its sheath, the shell racking home in the cold like precise steel biting. There is nothing more; an animal? A tree bursting? He crouches motionless, for if they are there they should be all around him, perhaps above on the cliff, and he will not move until he knows. Only the wind worrying spruce and snow, whining wordlessly. There, twenty yards away a shadow moves, Millen certainly, and his shot snaps as his rifle swings up, as he drops. Bullets snick from everywhere, their sound booming back and forth along the canyon. He has only fired once and is down, completely aware, on the wrong side of his fire and he shoots carefully again to draw their shots and they come, four harmlessly high and

150

nicely spaced out: there are two – Millen and another – below him in the canyon and two a bit higher on the right ridge, one of them that slipped. Nothing up the canyon or above on the cliff. With that knowledge he gathered himself and leaped over the fire against the cliff and one on the ridge made a good shot that cut his jacket and he could fall as if gut-shot in the hollow or deadfall. Until the fire died, he was almost comfortable.

In the growing dusk he watches the big Swede, who drove dogs very well, crawl toward Millen stretched out, face down. He watches him tie Millen's legs together with the laces of his mukluks and drag him backwards, plowing a long furrow and leaving the rifle sunk in the snow. He wastes no shot at their steady firing, and when they stop there are Millen's words still

You're surrounded. King isn't dead. Will you give

waiting, frozen in the canyon. He lay absolutely motionless behind the deadfall against the cliff, as if he were dead, knowing they would have to move finally. He flexed his feet continuously, and his fingers as he shifted the rifle no more quickly than a clock hand, moving into the position it would have to be when they charged him. They almost outwait him; it is really a question between the coming darkness and his freezing despite his invisible motions, but before darkness Millen had to move. Two of them were coming and he shifted his rifle slightly on the log to cover the left one – it must have been the long cold that made him mistake that for Millen – who dived out of sight, his shot thundering along the canyon, but Millen did not drop behind anything. Simply down on one knee, firing. Once, twice bullets tore the log and then he had his head up with those eyes staring straight down his sights and he fired two shots so fast the roar in the canyon sounded as one and Millen stood up, the whole length over him, whirled in that silent unmistakable way and crashed face down in the snow. He hears them dragging and chopping trees for a stage cache to keep the body, and in the darkness he chops handholds up the face of the cliff, step by step as he hoists himself and his pack out of another good shelter. As he has had to leave others.

3. *The Rat River,* N.W.T.: Saturday, January 10, 1932
Thursday, December 31, 1931
Tuesday, July 28

In his regular round of each loophole he peers down the promontory toward their fires glaring up from behind the riverbank. They surround him on three sides, nine of them with no more than forty dogs, which in this cold means they already need more supplies than they can have brought with them. They will be making plans for something, suddenly, beyond bullets against his logs and guns and it will have to come soon. In the long darkness, and he can wait far easier than they. Dynamite. If they have any more to thaw out very carefully after blowing open the roof and stovepipe as darkness settled, a hole hardly big enough for one of them – a Norwegian, they were everywhere with their long noses – to fill it an instant, staring down at him gathering himself from the corner out of roof-sod and pipes and snow: the cabin barely stuck above the drifts but that one was gigantic to lean in like that, staring until he lifted his rifle and the long face vanished an instant before his bullet passed through that space. But the hole was large enough for the cold to slide down along the wall and work itself into his trench, which would be all that saved him when they used the last of their dynamite. He began to feel what they had stalked him with all day: cold tightening steadily as steel around toes, face, around fingers.

In the clearing still nothing stirs. There is only the penumbra of light along the circle of the bank as if they had laid a trench-fire to thaw the entire promontory and were soundlessly burrowing in under him. Their flares were long dead, the sky across the river flickering with orange lights to vanish down into spruce and willows again, like the shadow blotting a notch in the eastern bank and he thrust his rifle through the chink and had almost got a shot away when a projectile arced against the sky and he jerked the gun out, diving, into the trench deep under the wall among the moose hides that could not protect him from the roof and walls tearing apart so loud it seemed most of himself had been blasted to the farthest granules of sweet, silent, earth. The sods and foot-thick logs he had built together where the river curled were gone and he would climb out and walk away as he always had, but first he pulled himself up and out between the splinters, still holding the rifle, just in time to see yellow light humpling through the snow toward him and he fired three times so fast it sounded in his ears as though his cabin was continuing to explode. The shadows around the light dance in one spot an instant but come on in a straight black line, lengthening down, faster, and the light cuts straight across his eyes and he gets away the fourth shot and the light tears itself into bits. He might have been lying on his back staring up into night and had the stars explode into existence above him. And whatever darkness is left before him then blunders away, desperately plowing away from him through the snow like the first one who came twice with a voice repeating at his door

I am Constable Alfred King, are you in there?

fist thudding the door the second time with a paper creaking louder than his voice so thin in the cold silence

I have a search warrant now, we have had complaints and if you don't open

and then plowing away in a long desperate scrabble through the sun-shot snow while the three others at the riverbank thumped their bullets hopelessly high into the logs but shattering the window again and again until they dragged King and each other head first over the edge while he placed lead carefully over them, snapping willow bits on top of them and still seeing, strangely, the tiny hole that had materialized up into his door when he flexed the trigger, still hearing the grunt that had wormed in through the slivers of the board he had whipsawn himself. Legs and feet wrapped in moose hide lay a moment across his window, level in the snow, jerking as if barely attached to a body knocked over helpless, a face somewhere twisted in gradually developing pain that had first leaned against his door, fist banging while that other one held the dogs at the edge of the clearing, waiting

Hallo? Hallo? This is Constable Alfred King of the Royal Canadian Mounted Police. I want to talk to you. Constable Millen

and they looked into each other's eyes, once, through his tiny window. The eyes peering down into his – could he be seen from out of the blinding sun? – squinted blue from a boy's round face with a bulging nose bridged over pale with cold. King, of the Royal Mounted. Like a silly book title, or the funny papers. He didn't look it as much as Spike Millen, main snooper and tracker

153

at Arctic Red River who baked pies and danced, everybody said, better than any man in the north. Let them dance hipped in snow, get themselves dragged away under spruce and dangling traps, asking, laying words on him, naming things

> You come across from the Yukon? You got a trapper's licence? The Loucheaux trap the Rat, up towards the Richardson Mountains. You'll need a licence, why not

Words. Dropping out of nothing into advice. Maybe he wanted a kicker to move that new canoe against the Rat River? Loaded down as it is. The Rat drops fast, you have to hand-line the portage anyway to get past Destruction City where those would-be Klondikers wintered in '98. He looked up at the trader above him on the wedge of gravel. He had expected at least silence. From a trader standing with the bulge of seven hundred dollars in his pocket; in the south a man could feed himself with that for two years. Mouths always full of words, pushing, every mouth falling open and dropping words from nothing into meaning. The trader's eyes shifted finally, perhaps to the junction of the rivers behind them, south and west, the united river clicking under the canoe. As he raised his paddle. The new rifle oiled and ready with its butt almost touching his knees as he kneels, ready to pull the canoe around.

4. *Above Fort McPherson,* N.W.T.: Tuesday, July 7, 1931

The Porcupine River, as he thought it was then, chuckled between the three logs of his raft. He could hear that below him, under the mosquitoes probing the mesh about his head, and see the gold lengthen up the river like the canoe that would come toward him from the north where the sun just refused to open the spiky horizon. Gilded, hammered out slowly, soundlessly toward him the thick gold. He sat almost without breathing, watching it come like silence. And then imperceptibly the black spired riverbend grew pointed, stretched itself in a thin straight line double-bumped, gradually spreading a straight wedge below the sun through the golden river. When he had gathered that slowly into anger it was already too late to choke his fire; the vee had abruptly bent toward him, the bow man already raised his paddle; hailed. Almost it seemed as if a name had been blundered into the silence, but he did not move in his fury. The river chuckled again.

154

" . . . o-o-o-o . . . " the point of the wedge almost under him now. And the sound of a name, that was so clear he could almost distinguish it. Perhaps he already knew what it was, had long since lived this in that endlessly enraged chamber of himself, even to the strange Indian accent mounded below him in the canoe bow where the black hump of the stern partner moved them straight toward him out of the fanned ripples, crumpling gold. To the humps of his raft below on the gravel waiting to anchor them.

"What d'ya want."

"You Albert Johnson?"

It could have been the sternman who named him. The sun like hatchet-strokes across slanted eyes, the gaunt noses below him there holding the canoe against the current, their paddles hooked in the logs of his raft. Two Loucheaux half-faces, black and red kneeling in the roiled gold of the river, the words thudding softly in his ears.

You Albert Johnson?

One midnight above the Arctic Circle to hear again the inevitability of name. He has not heard it in four years, it could be to the very day since that Vancouver garden, staring into the evening sun and hearing this quiet sound from these motionless – perhaps they are men kneeling there, perhaps waiting for him to accept again what has now been laid inevitably upon him, the name come to meet him in his journey north, come out of north around the bend and against the current of the Peel River, as they name that too, to confront him on a river he thought another and aloud where he would have found after all his years, at long last, only nameless silence.

You Albert Johnson?

"Yes," he said finally.

And out of his rage he begins to gather words together. Slowly, every word he can locate, as heavily as he would gather stones on a Saskatchewan field, to hold them for one violent moment against himself between his two hands before he heaves them up and hurls them – but they are gone. The ripples of their passing may have been smoothing out as he stares at where they should have been had they been there. Only the briefly golden river lies before him, whatever its name may be since it must have one, bending back somewhere beyond that land, curling back upon itself in its giant, relentless spirals down to the implacable, and ice-choked, arctic sea.

155

Note on the Author

Rudy Wiebe, whose 1973 novel from McClelland and Stewart, *The Temptations of Big Bear*, was named winner of the Governor General's Award for Fiction, was born in 1934 in northern Saskatchewan. He received his early education at the Alberta Mennonite High School in Coaldale, attended the University of Alberta (B.A., M.A., English), studied for a year at the University of Tuebingen, West Germany under a Rotary International Fellowship, took classes in teacher education at the University of Manitoba and taught high school briefly. He has been editor of the *Mennonite Brethern Herald* and has taught at Goshen College, Indiana. Currently, he is Associate Professor of Canadian Literature and Creative Writing at the University of Alberta in Edmonton, where he lives with his wife and three children.

Short stories, reviews, essays and articles by Rudy Wiebe have been published in numerous literary magazines in Canada and the United States. He has prepared radio documentaries for the C.B.C. and his adaptation of his second novel, *First and Vital Candle,* was produced on C.B.C. radio in 1967.

Acknowledgements

These stories originally appeared
in the following publications:

New Liberty Magazine, *Christian Living*,
Tamarack Review, *Fiddlehead*, *The Mennonite*,
First and Vital Candle, *The Star-Spangled Beaver*,
Prism international, *White Pelican*,
Fourteen Stories High and *Queen's Quarterly*;
several were also read on C.B.C. Anthology.